Gerardo di Masso

The Shadow by the Door

translated by
Richard Jacques

CURBSTONE PRESS

For Maria Elena, Raquel and Claudia.
For Tato.
From here, hardly even that.

First U. S. Edition
The Shadow by the Door was was first published in this translation by Zed Books Ltd., London, in 1985.
La Penumbra by Gerardo di Masso was originally published in Spanish by Ediciones Ttarttalo, San Sebastian, Spain, in 1983.

ISBN: 0-915306-78-6
LC Number: 87-73441

This publication was supported in part by The Connecticut Commission on the Arts, a State Agency whose funds are recommended by the Governor and appropriated by the State Legislature and in part by the contributions of numerous individuals.

distributed in the U.S. by
The Talman Co., 150 Fifth Ave., New York, NY 10011

CURBSTONE PRESS, 321 Jackson Street, Willimantic, CT 06226

Translator's Preface

The country of the book is never named and though we can infer Argentina, it could unhappily be any of the countries of the Southern Cone of the Latin American Continent. If we, like Luis, have trouble 'believing the truth of this whole fiction', we need only consult the report produced in 1984 by CONADEP, the *Comisión Nacional sobre Desaparición de las Personas*, or National Committee for Missing Persons, under the Presidency of Ernesto Sábato. The report is the fruit – if we can use such a word in the context – of a long and terrible labour, the endeavour to discover the fate of the missing, *'los desaparecidos'*, a word which has sadly become universal currency. It was compiled from the testimony of the few who survived the torture chambers, their friends and relatives and even some of the repressors themselves, who had, for whatever reasons, come forward to tell what they knew. The Committee was able to confirm about 9,000 cases, but there were certainly many more, not declared at the time for fear of reprisals. Even under the new democratic government, people still fear to come forward, in terror of a return to power of what Sábato unhesitatingly calls 'the forces of evil'.

It is difficult to read the report without disbelief. Not only because the figures themselves are unbelievable, and because the range of victims is quite wide enough to have included anyone reading this preface had they had the misfortune to be in Argentina at the time, but also because of the imagination and inventiveness of the torturers. And yet these were – are – men, like the man in the book with his wife and family and flower garden. In one case of which I have personal knowledge, the kidnappers, having removed the 'suspect' to torture and death, proceeded to ransack the house, removing, amongst other things, the toys which had been given, that same day, to his daughter for her eleventh birthday. Presumably as gifts for their own children.

The great strength of fiction is that it is warm where statistics are cold. In *The Shadow by the Door*, we live through the torment of Xavier, Marta and Carlos and we travel with Luis on the road through the winter mountains. Memory dominates the book: as the protagonists struggle to retain their sanity in the torture chambers, they retreat into a country of the mind, the past, with its healing memories of childhood, of love, of nature, of everything which gives life. This is all they can oppose to the darkness and despair of their world behind the blindfold. Luis too reflects constantly on the past – the past of his childhood and youth, which he shares with his brother and friends who are beyond his help; the past of his political activity; and the historical past of South America itself. At one of the finest moments in the book, he 'becomes' the Indian lying in ambush for the Spanish horsemen and perceives the heart of the 'tireless struggle' between the forces of life and creation and those of death and destruction. The Conquistadors 'will come back out of nowhere, riding their horses and hurling themselves into combat with their crosses and their banners'. Sábato speaks of the terminology of repression; the crusade against 'materialists and atheists, enemies of Western Christian values', in the words of the ideologues of the 'Dirty War'.

The translation of this book was a labour of love and hope. Love for friends who suffered in Argentina and later in exile and who still suffer in the memory of the black years. Hope that we can learn to see beyond the waste and stupidity of the Malvinas/Falklands war and do whatever is within our power to assist the survival of the fragile democracy. To quote again from Sábato:

> Great calamities are always instructive, and what was undoubtedly the most terrible experience undergone by the nation in the whole of its history during the period of the military dictatorship which began in March 1976 will help us to understand that democracy alone is capable of

preserving a people from such horror, that it alone can safeguard and uphold the sacred and essential rights of human beings. Only in this way can we be sure that our country will never see a repetition of the events which have made us tragically famous throughout the civilised world.

Translator's Note

I regret the sacrifice of the title, *La Penumbra*, but whereas the word 'penumbra' is in everyday usage in Spanish, in English it seemed to me over technical. In relinquishing it, I had to lose the richness of its overtones of ambiguity, the area between darkness and light. But all translation is approximation, and involves loss of one kind or another. The gain is the accessibility of a work to a far greater audience. I hope that this version gives at least an idea of the beauty of the original.

Richard Jacques

He was there, as always, leaning against the wall. The room was almost empty, scarcely any light on the walls and the floor. A silence of empty vases shattering against the windows and the doors. The solitary old house, the garden overrun with weeds and broken bottles, the weather-vane motionless in a wind which had passed by long ago. The feeble morning light drew figures in the dust on the ceiling and moved them slowly through the man's restless memory. A distant roll of thunder vibrated the still air, more rain, he thought, the same as ever on this same journey from a house fading into an infinite expanse of country to the frozen peaks of the solitary snow-swept mountains. From the silent streets, the headlong flight of a car, four phantoms clinging to their weapons and the last gesture of someone falling in slow motion on to the wet asphalt.

The story was the invisible thread inexorably linking the rusty windmill and the lifeless siesta in the small town, the smell of freshly-baked bread and the symmetry of the fences, a pale face and two plaits looking north, waiting for the rain and another tired face, your own, looking south through the wall. And, in between, the slow journey, all the roads, the comrades lying dead under the placid gaze of life, the tortured, broken bodies in dark, underground places, all the hope and all the sadness.

I remember them alive, he murmured, because that is the only way for me to keep believing in the truth of this whole fiction. I will take them back with me, take them back with me and the journey will be over.

1

He lit a cigarette, looked back at the terracotta figures which were staring at him from the shelf and remembered the exhausting days under a sun like a sniper in an open, cloudless sky, not even a strip of shadow to lie down in and snatch a little sleep or just rest the bones. There was nothing. Not even a late bird flying through the scrub.

A patch of damp cut the wall in two and a huge cockroach scurried along the skirting board, lost and hungry. A thousand million years old, he thought, those creatures will be here when all this is just a memory, a charred shadow, they will be here devouring corpses and bricks.

What has become of them, he wondered, what happened to them after the ambush, and you've got no answer because you were petrified, crouching behind an embankment listening to the shots, the shouts, the blows, the silence. A broken rifle in your hands and Montero behind a tree stopping you with a look. And now the waiting is coming to an end in this bare house, in this frozen winter you can feel through the shattered window panes like an intake of icy breath, which probes the teeth and sets them off in an uncontrollable stammer.

She never knew, and today the memory is just a scrap of paper with a few hastily scribbled words and her, naked at the foot of the bed with one blue stocking and the outstretched arms that will never find you now. So all loneliness begins and there will be no redemption, no forgetting, no territory, only a second to escape into the fog and vanish on the other side of the hill following the line of the stream, a trickle of water which looked like a steel snake crawling under the sun.

October had gone by through the trees and they had orders to separate, break ranks, vanish into some city, some village hidden in the mountains until the danger had passed and you could face her and tell her that you could not take another single step, that it would be best to leave it at that, that it had been beautiful while it had lasted and that you would always keep the memory of the love that was falling into the abyss like a rifle shot vanishing into the shadows of the mountain.

The rainy season was hurling water down on to the parched earth. The men had been feeling its merciless pounding for several weeks as they headed north, sweating, exhausted and drenched, in search of the other column which had set out from Los Sauces and had already had one encounter on the banks of the Santa Margarita river. 'You can't leave it all like this,' she said, clinging to the window frame to keep herself from falling into the oblivion that she was beginning to guess at from the clothes he was throwing into the old brown leather suitcase, 'you can't just go out like this and vanish as if everything we know had never existed, you can't.'

The path was hardly wide enough for them to move in single file, surrounded by tall reeds dripping with dirty, stinking water. The march was slow because the thick boots, caked with mud, weighed a ton and the rucksacks seemed to grow as they and the evening trudged on towards the horizon. Roque brought up the rear and tried to cover their tracks by dragging a large canvas bag which he carried slung from his belt, as if it were possible to disguise the passage of forty men along the narrow path which sucked in their footsteps and left them deeply imprinted like little graves of mud and straw.

'It's not that, you'll never understand, I have to go, leave, disappear, they're waiting for me and I haven't a minute to lose, I'm sorry, maybe we'll meet again some day, maybe, but I can't promise anything. I don't know myself how all this will end but I have to go and I don't want you to ask me any more questions, I'm sorry, really.' He kissed her lightly on the lips and opened the door.

2

'The column should already be somewhere around here, though,' said Valentin, pointing with his pencil to a wide area on the map surrounding the small airfield at Lobillos and indicating an arc which ended on the main road from Tampaya to the village of El Manzano. At that very moment Fermin had been shot below the shoulder blade and he was dead before he hit the ground. The night before, he had gone to sleep gazing at the moon, not knowing that a bullet was already waiting for him, to eat his blood with a single bite.

The next move was an orderly retreat to the east in groups of seven with two water bottles each, rationing the water and the dried salted meat which was hardly enough for one wretched meal for a shipwrecked sailor in that room which was all we had. One bed, two chairs, a few books and you getting up every morning at seven to go to work at the factory. Every day except Sunday. On Sundays we went to the river and stood on the quay watching the fishermen, the boats with strange flags from strange far-off countries where we would never go. Then we would wander back through the silent streets, our arms around each other, almost contented, almost happy, before packing the rucksacks and going out into the clearing that opened up like a threatening mouth, with the edge of the jungle three hundred yards away, the distance that would have to be covered at a run with both hands clutching the heart to keep it from bursting.

The battle lasted just over half an hour. Three wounded, Anselmo, Roque and Manuel. Perhaps a few wounded or even a couple dead among the Regulars, we broke through the cordon and plunged into the thick of the woods almost crawling, bumping into the low branches and startling the great multicoloured birds which flew off with screeches that could be heard far away like an omen.

She was left behind, her body leaning against an open door, two fists clenched in a gesture of impotence, almost of despair, as if to say some day you will come back in search of your memories.

3

It was an absurd clutching at hope, the bank sheer to the muddy river and six men trying to wade it while the current grew more violent, sweeping away tree trunks, stones, dead animals and branches with a thunderous roar which was almost lost among the mountains, but broke out again when the river was joined by its fast flowing tributary, the Pircas. A rope kept them precariously upright between two banks which moved with the current in a mixture of sand and sludge, of crushed flowers and lily pads eaten away by bugs and worms. Carmelo went first, then Bastos, Aguirre, Biri the Kid, Montero and El Alto who brought up the rear of the pathetic line of amphibians. It was already almost dark and the rain fell unabated, beating relentlessly on their exhausted faces, soaking their webbing and faded combat uniforms. It was like a nightmare, a scene from hell, but a hell which was flooded, dripping and unreal. And yet they were there, creeping forward step by step in search of a break in the dense jungle, the slightest sign of a path between the green walls which were swallowing them up. And behind them the Regulars with their huge grey capes which transformed them into dark phantoms, an army marching without a compass on the heels of other men who did not have one either, in a macabre game which seemed as if it would never end. Some of them thought that a single bullet was killing all of them. The rain kept on and behind the window panes the street was a great pool that reflected the lights of the cars, the quick shadows of the people who had ventured out in the storm, her figure, hunched and running to the doorway of the house and up the stairs two at a time, flying into the little room to tell you that you seemed strange, far away, and there was Aguirre waving his arms and shouting that there was a small opening where they could climb the bank and then a path, to tell you that she was going to make coffee, 'I'm frozen,' she added.

4

'You're going to talk, they all talk sooner or later, I can wait all night, all week, for ever, it's always a matter of time and I've got time, you know that's how it is, it had to happen one day, you can't live hiding like rats, though that's what you are, stinking rats, bastards, fucking cowardly murderers, that's what you are, and I'm going to tear your guts out if you don't spill, I'm going to tear them out anyway, those are the rules of the game, you cunt, and I've got a job to do, because this is my job, information, the search for information, collecting facts, names, dates, addresses, streets, cities, movements, and I'm good at what I do, some people say I'm the best, the bosses are pleased with me, I've got a clean slate, no blots on my copybook, sooner or later, I've already told you, it hurts, of course it hurts, it can't be nice to have your fingernails pulled out with a pair of pliers, go on scream, nobody's going to hear you, come on, I want to hear those names, OK, if you don't want to talk that's your funeral, but you've got to realise that I have a job to do, you know something I need to know and they want me to find out, it's obvious, you gambled and lost, you've still got eight finger-nails and the night's young, it's up to you, you talk or you'll end up as garbage, as shit, as nothing, you know, who are they, where are they, when were you going to meet them, what are they planning in the city, come on, I'm waiting, seven nails, I don't think you'll get to the fifth before you faint, you're all pansies, you drop faster than a tart's knickers, if you talked it would all be a lot easier, a bit of a working over and off to jail, but this is no good, go on Cardozo, another nail off the hero, they're all the same, they pass out just as the party's swinging, take him away, we'll carry on tomorrow, we've still got the other hand and all the time in the world.'

5

When he was a boy his uncle Pedro used to take him to the country; he came to fetch him in town at six in the morning and they travelled along lonely dirt roads until they reached the huge, tumbledown old house where Fabian still lived with his wife, La Prude. There were chickens and ducks, two enormous dogs and a few cats which spent their lives running away from the snapping jaws of El Tigre and Nero. Several horses grazed gloomily in the distance and the frogs hid among the water-cress in the brook. Most of all, he remembered the summers, Luis and Javier, the endless siestas under the deadly sun, the lizards scuttling by and the sound of the windmill turning half-heartedly in the feeble breeze that blew from the south. He remembered the summers for Teresa, Teresa's plaits, the games with Teresa in the old shed where they kept the seeds and the tools. He thought the memory made him invulnerable, that it was enough to drive away pain and sadness. Later he found out that it was not true, but he never forgot her, could never forget the black eyes, surprised by the first kiss and the first caress, he could never forget that trembling urgency of young naked bodies in a dry straw loft, and the smell of Teresa, her wonderful smell of fresh grass, of dew, of butter on hot bread at breakfast, he could never forget that he had been an onlooker while she and Luis moved on the sacks of wheat, locked in each other's arms, he could never forget that. He looked at his left hand, a bleeding mass which semed to have grown like a monstrous shape invading his arm and making him groan with pain when he tries to stand up in the narrow cell to shake off the terrors of the night, the frightful creatures blending with the bricks of the wall and spawning among the flagstones, the names he has almost forgotten by denying and resisting the pain, the blows, the electricity eating up his body, his testicles, his tongue, his teeth, his memory. He did not know how much time had passed, he did not know what day it was, he did not know where he was, he only knew that the game was coming to an end, that he could not hold out much longer, that everything has a limit and he was reaching it, he had almost set foot on the last scream, the last tear, the last glance at Teresa one afternoon in February when he told her he was going to live in the City and that he would write to her.

6

When they reached the hedge, they split up into two groups of three and started to move slowly forward between the high meadows which almost hid the entrance to the house. The rain had stopped, but the sky was still grey and the clouds were gathering in the west, as if waiting. Marcos, who had joined them on the third day of the march, rolled a cigarette with the shred of dry tobacco he had left and put it between his lips without lighting it, made a gesture and the two groups advanced in an encircling movement that momentarily silenced the song of the birds.

The house seemed deserted; the stillness was visible. In the remaining light, Roque ran across the courtyard and up to one of the windows and peered inside. A clap of thunder shook the sky and the rain began to fall monotonously. Roque signalled them to come on, leaned against the wall and took off his cap. He was exhausted, in pain, dropping with sleep. So were they all and they still had forty miles to go before they met up with Lino and the others. They forced the door open and went in. There was just one rickety table and a few broken chairs, a staircase to the upper floor and a fireplace with two half-burned logs. The wood was damp and they could see that the last occupant had abandoned the house a long time before. Night was falling and they had to gather dry wood to endure the cold for the next few days. In the season it could rain for months on end until it seemed that the whole area was one immense raindrop drowning the seeds in the gound and driving people from their homes, laying waste with a liquid hand and pursuing them to a grave in some gorge lost in the mountains.

They posted sentries, managed eventually to light a small fire and got ready to rest. El Alto went upstairs and lay down on a rusty bedstead that someone had covered with a ludicrous piece of worn out, foul-smelling cloth. He crossed his hands under his head and stared at the ceiling until sleep began to carry him away. Far away from there, between the sound of the rain and the wind rattling the mouldy blinds.

7

He was walking down a deserted street and the sun was blazing relentlessly down on the dazzling, immaculate whitewashed walls. He did not know exactly where he was but he had a disturbing feeling, sense, presentiment or foreboding of having been there before, in this street, with this hard, motionless but almost liquid sun. He was walking in slow motion, the sweat running down his back and sticking the shirt to his armpits, great salty drops cascading down and forming a mist over his eyes, and the hard ground burned his feet. He was barefoot and his trousers were held up by a string. He was walking but scarcely moving, the heat was beating on his head and scorching his brain, the street was deserted and he could have sworn he had been there before, some time, long, long ago. El Alto was dreaming, sprawled on the bare bedstead, breathing through his half-open mouth and moving his hand as if trying to protect himself. Suddenly his muscles tensed under the skin, his jaw contracted in a savage rictus, the nightmare was taking shape, the first outlines of its old sleeping venom, the sun kept up its relentless pursuit and the first group appeared at the corner, the vanguard, a pale squadron of skeletons who walked pressed against the wall, wearing shreds of ancient imperial uniforms, the remains of faded blue neckerchiefs gnawed away by vultures and crows, by rats and flies. Other skeletons came behind them, their bones almost transparent, their skulls slightly bowed as if in greeting. It was a solemn parade and El Alto was surprised to see that the strange army cast no shadow, he could observe its absence on the walls and on the scorched ground. He stood stock still while the parade vanished along other streets, under the same sun, without the same shadow. Then he woke up, his mouth parched and his bladder bursting. He got up, went to the toilet, urinated, looked at his tired face in the mirror and went back to the room. She was asleep, one foot sticking out from under the blanket, a lock of fair hair partly covering one eye. Beautiful, he thought, she is beautiful and she will be left alone, completely alone. He had begun to miss her and there were still several days left before the journey began.

Day was breaking. He went to the kitchen and sipped a glass of water, looked out of the window and saw the sun, an orange blot far away, a round hand peeping over the rim of the sky.

8

Anselmo and Manuel were recovering from their wounds. Roque was already better. He was a bull, Roque, strong and hard, made of stone. Anselmo's leg was healing quickly and the hole in Manuel's shoulder was scarcely noticeable under the bandage. Dawn had broken four hours earlier, but the mountain fog still had not cleared, a thick curtain of damp which stopped miraculously a yard above the ground and hovered there, waiting. Activity in the house was relaxed. Montero was cleaning his rifle with a dirty rag which he had kept since the retreat in August, 'I bent down to pick it up and just at that moment a bullet buried itself in the tree trunk above my head, above my life, I'd say.' Aguirre was playing chess by himself with strange chessmen that he had made from breadcrumbs on a board of cork burnt to mark the squares. 'I always lose,' he said, 'maybe tomorrow my luck will change.' Biri the Kid, the Lefthanded Gun, a strange nickname for a man with only one arm, the right arm, is standing by the window staring out as if from there, from the pane looking out on to the thick mist, he could see the sea, a sea which accompanies his every word, 'I was born in La Coba, in a boat my uncle kept to carry contraband to Puerto Encarnacion, my parents lived on the boat and while they were there they looked after the old man, Don Blas, the Gringo Captain, my grandfather, the smuggler, the best man in the world. If you're born in La Coba you're doomed, you need the sea to move, to breathe, to learn to eat, to suffer, for ever.'

Biri stared through the window at the sea which was not there and Bastos stirred a thick, dark soup which was cooking in an immense black pot perched on the wood fire. El Alto was still asleep upstairs and the fog was beginning to lift like a bird taking flight. The door opened and Valentin came in, 'Someone's coming,' he said, 'you can't see very well, but it might be a patrol of Regulars. Put out the fire, wake El Alto, take up positions at the windows, wait.' The morning was changing course, the mist fled with the wind behind it, the first shot was fired. El Alto leapt off the bed, grabbed the rifle, flattened himself against the wall and saw the granary, the weather-vane topping the roof of the house, Javier and Carlos bathing in the pond, saw the uppermost branches of the paradise trees behind the mill and there, in the distance, the Chavez's shed, Teresa's parents. He stayed pressed against the flaking plaster of the room and a bullet shattered the window frame. He tried to look out and another shot removed the last bits of wood and putty, a shard of glass and two spiders' webs which vanished with a bang as if in a conjuring trick. He looked out again and this time he could see a flight of ducks to the south, a tight delta formation, the drake in the centre, the younger ducks behind him, then the females and the old ducks bringing up the rear of a flight that might end in a sudden hail of bullets like a many fingered hand which would drag them down to the mirror of the lake, among the reeds, towards the dogs. He also saw a thick column of smoke over in the direction of the town and imagined the fire, the wheat, parched by the sun, falling before the onset of the flames, the ears of corn turned into little tongues hanging from the blackened stalks. The fieldmice hidden in their nests suffocated by the smoke; he imagined the spectacle of a harvest burning in the middle of the night and realised that it was not a fire, just the chimney of a cheese factory where they occasionally burnt green branches to drive off the mosquitoes. That was it, the smoke was coming in through the shattered window and El Alto realised that the house was on fire. He heard voices from downstairs and a shout, 'Alto, let's go, the house is on fire, we've got to get out of here.' He went down the stairs three at a time, reached the door and could just make out a few figures deformed by the blue and grey smoke, blurred shapes running for the river, tracks in the air, and started to run.

9

There was a street lamp on the corner near the house but it had gone out. Somebody had smashed the bulb with a well-aimed stone and now the district was in total darkness. The only light filtered through the windows of Santiago's bar, but it shut at eleven and at ten past it was like the black mouth of a black wolf. It was raining that night and the three cars pulled up near the third house, a single-storey building painted light green, with a little garden at the front and a hedge intertwined with wistaria. It was two in the morning and they started to get out, unconcerned about the noise of the doors closing. Nine men who made for the entrance, then separated, and five of them went round to the back through a dark alley giving on to a piece of waste ground. Three others stayed at the wheels of the cars, their guns bulging under their armpits and their belts. One of them lit a cigarette, gulped down a lungful of poisonous black smoke, spat out a shred of tobacco and drummed on the steering wheel with his fists. 'It's hot,' he thought, 'God knows when I'll be through with this and go home and get into a tub full of iced water with a beer in each hand, I'd like that,' he thought, while the others were kicking the door down, rushing into the house and dragging the man and the woman out, pushing and punching them, thrusting them into a car and leaving two children crying in the shattered doorway, alone.

It was starting to rain again and the three cars were just another shadow, already far away from the sobbing and the wistaria.

10

He ran desperately, gasping for breath, his heart in his mouth, stumbled, fell and ran on again, dragging his exhaustion along the river bank. He could see Bastos hiding in a bend of the river protected by a few yellow reeds that stuck out of the water like fingers. He passed by him and saw that Aguirre was there too, the two of them were setting up the heavy machine-gun against some stones and beginning to load it. He crossed the stream by a rickety wood and rope bridge and ran on into the jungle to rejoin Montero at the foot of an immense banana tree. 'The others,' he asked, 'where are they?' Montero pointed into the depths of the jungle, 'We'll join them tomorrow evening at the Stone House, now we've got to move on, Bastos and Aguirre will cover us till dusk, then they'll head south, come on, there's no time to lose.' The jungle became thicker and thicker, suffocating, impenetrable. The great trees grew upwards in search of the sky, stopping half way, cut off by other trees which had arrived before, searching for light, offering the birds their topmost branches to make their nests, adorning their crowns with starlight and raindrops. Down below, a strange mass of vegetation crowded among the thick trunks, jostling to drink the liquid that was rightfully theirs, straining for a view of the landscape which they never managed to see. That was the jungle, the height and the sky. Soon the first shadows fell and the dense foliage was filled with sounds, dull noises of wood and beak and wings. They prepared to spend the night in a small clearing which they hacked out with machetes, ate cold meat and a scrap of dry bread, drank half a canteen of water and slept. It was a clear night with a full moon; a gentle breeze wandered among the trees, you kissed her slowly on the mouth, holding time still between your tongue, you told her something with your hands, pressed yourself against her waist and she understood.

11

He had stayed up reading the book that Paco had lent him that evening. 'Read it, you'll like it, the writer isn't famous but it's very gripping, it's a good thriller, the baddies win.' The family was asleep, Marta snuggled up to the pillow and the children uncovered, the three of them in the big bed, silence in the whole house, little Ana's fair hair tied up with a red ribbon, Luisito's black curls, the pyjamas that were already too small for him, you took them to their beds, covered Marta gently and went back to the living-room to carry on reading. Sleep began to crawl over you like a silkworm, you put the book down, went to get a glass of water, drank it, went to the lavatory and got into bed. It had been raining all day and it was still drumming on the courtyard among the flower pots, it would lull you to sleep as if the bed were on the banks of a mountain stream; you closed your eyes, and then you heard the first footsteps, the squeak of rubber soles on the tiles in the corridor, the unintelligible muttering of voices, the certainty that they were there, the crack as the lock on the door was smashed, the masked faces under the woollen hats, the rifles and pistols, the screams of the children, the terror of Marta who was only half awake, realising that this was the nightmare, these sinister men who had shattered the silence, who were seizing them brutally by the arms and punching them as they dragged them towards the black mouth of the night through the door hanging off its hinges. You even had time to look at her, knowing that you would never forget that terrified face, that wordless glance that asked a thousand questions that you could not answer. You even had time to hear Luisito cry out in anguish and Ana sobbing, you wanted to wrench yourself free and run back to hug them, protect them, tell them it was all a bad dream, to go back to bed, but then came the blow on the back of the head and the night went darker and the shouts seemed farther off and you knew you were fainting as they pushed you into a car and she was calling your name a thousand miles away.

12

'Don't wait for me today in the usual place, I don't know how long I'll be out of town. Yesterday I got a short message to say we were leaving, I'm already on my way as I write these few lines to say a hasty goodbye. Don't worry, any more than you have to, I mean. Take care of yourself, I'll send news. Do take care of yourself, please, we'll meet again, we both know that. Luis.'

She crumpled the paper in her fist and burnt it carefully in the ashtray full of nub ends and cold ash. She put her hands on the table, leaned her head on her shoulder and watched the goodbye go slowly up in smoke. She sat still for a long time, silent, not moving. A tear trickled down her cheek, past her nose to the corner of her mouth. That was all. 'Goodbye, then,' she said softly, and left.

13

The night was pitch dark. Montero slept leaning against a big black rock which he had padded with the groundsheet, using the rucksack as a pillow and covering himself with the old oilskin. A sticky damp rose from the grass, penetrated his bones and clung there, soaking through to his guts and frightening sleep away. El Alto crossed the little clearing they had carved out with the blades of their machetes, squatted down by a thicket and listened, trying to peer through the dense foliage, came back and sat down by a tree, his rifle between his legs, his knife in his right boot, took out a cigarette, hid the flame between his hands and lit it, took a few puffs, looked at the starry sky and felt all the concentrated exhaustion of days and nights escaping death by inches, fleeing through a strange land where everything was confused and the days seemed far longer than in the City. He could not remember when all this business had begun; he only knew that he could never forget that interminable journey, the wretched villages scattered along the railway lines, the little stations by the side of the tracks, the ramshackle truck that left him on the border, the long walk in the sun, the meeting with Martin and El Palido, the first meal on the mountain, the loneliness dawning on the face that was imagining his departure, as she read the few stark words of farewell, and a sharp pain in the stomach that had never left him since.

Montero was snoring heavily and shaking in his sleep, perhaps from memories that had been waiting patiently for the moment to creep aboard and dump their melancholy load. He turned over on the narrow stone, brushed a mosquito off his face and snored on until dawn.

Now they were on the way, two grey blobs heading north through the heart of the leaves, nothing more.

14

He had kissed her hands as a point of departure, he had kissed her arms slowly and worked his way up to her eyelids almost without a pause, he had caressed her whole body with his fingers. He opened his eyes; the room was lit by a dim, yellowish bulb hanging from the ceiling over a corner where he could see a little black instrument and a long cable disappearing into the wall at the end of the room; he could see a man in shirt-sleeves holding one end of the wire, testing the tiny round point, lightly brushing the nipple that swelled at the touch of his finger tips, under the gentle pressure of his thumb and first finger, until it was like a promontory surrounded by a warm, pink nimbus, feeling the other hand coming close and discovering the hot little point eating into your palate, wandering over your teeth and lingering on your tongue until it choked your groans down your throat, travelling through the saliva and leaving little kisses on all her beauty spots, exploring her body from head to toe, visiting her sex and starting over again from an unimaginable height. The man works scientifically, chooses his spots and moves the point towards the areas where pain is an uncrossable frontier, where tears are just a pretext to discharge a little of the terror while the electricity alights on his penis and turns it into an appalling vehicle carrying millions of wounds inside his flesh and her hand on his testicles, caressing them tenderly, bringing her tongue up to the huge glans which she hides inside her mouth and caresses with her lips, licks with the tip of her tongue and with the fierce tip which attacks his armpits, destroying any possible resistance as it passes, stabs into his ears and descends towards his navel, fast, like a bird of prey hovering above its victim. Then she lifts her legs and wraps them around your waist, hugging you with her heels against the hardness of your ribs, clings like someone shipwrecked to the wooden plank of your sex and draws you towards her and you fall with an atrocious pain in the back, in the anus, the furious tip has bitten you there, treacherously, breaking you inside as if you were a piece of china, has torn a heartrending scream from your throat and arched your back like a reed lashed by the wind, she has plunged you inside her with a single movement of her wonderful hips, buried one sex inside the other, lain back on the sheets and started to gyrate her belly in circles, in a dance that drives you wild, started to suck your juices knowing that you are at her mercy, but you are not going to talk, you are not going to answer a single question, you are going to wipe that smirk off his face while you thrust down on her like a madman plunging in and out and in again, the saliva and the groans mingled together, the movements and the laboured gasps and the bulging eyes staring at a distant point in the centre of the ceiling until the last cry, the contorted scream of the orgasm of oblivion.

15

He was cold. He felt a procession of freezing ants crawling over his body, not missing a single pore, a birthmark, the scars. Winter crept between the flagstones, through the concrete bench easily penetrating the dirty palliasse and bit into him from every side, froze him slowly all over while up above the broken pane of a small window with three bars let in the night like a hand which opened and wafted out the constant, icy wind, the other torture, his sleep broken and his skin barely covered by a thin, short-sleeved shirt, his trousers in rags and his feet bare.

He did not know where he was; he could hear distant sounds, a car engine, a horn, an aeroplane, silence and cries, the cries that accompanied the enforced insomnia, the appalling symphony that came in through cracks and broke against the damp walls of the cell, the familiar sound of groans, the feeble yellowish light that fades when the cables are plugged in, the screams and the silence; dawn.

He went over to the door and heard the footsteps and the obscenities, the feet dragging on the uneven floor, the slamming of a door, the rattle of the key in the lock and the bolt drawn back, the noise of a body falling a few yards away, separated by a wall which does not manage complete separation, but hints at the presence of the other person, the beaten flesh, the blood, the slow return to consciousness, the ridiculous joy of finding oneself alive and the sudden certainty of the unknown, the night and the silence, especially the silence, now that they have gone away.

Three quick raps with the knuckles on the sandy surface of the wall, a long interval and three more raps, then four, now two, just one sharp tap. Somebody is trying to make contact with me, you mutter between your battered lips, somebody wants me to know they are there, but I can't move, I'm nailed down in this hole and I'm pissing myself and my heart's freezing and somebody is knocking, again, three knocks, four, one, silence. Now you get up with a movement that takes centuries and your hand trembles towards the wall, closing painfully in a fist that knocks, almost delicately, brushing the bricks and falling back alongside the body, gathering strength and knocking again, almost loud this time, three times, two, one. He's answering, he's there and he's heard you, he's alive and mangled like you, the same chill gnawing at his flesh, in the same night, in this nightmare.

He thought about Marta, it couldn't be her, they'd be keeping her somewhere else, they'd be doing the same things to her, they'd leave him alone here so that he'd think she was a long way away or imagine that she was nearby, but they wouldn't let him see her, just let his imagination fill in the details of the scenes and the people, the decor and the dialogue, her face with the same wordless question in her eyes, the empty cry for the children in the endless distance, the pain of not knowing where she was although he knew that the taps would not bring her from the other side of the wall. He preferred to imagine her on another planet and not behind those taps, beyond that grey wall like an abyss. You spoke her name leaning back against the shadows and a terrible feeling of desolation closed your eyes, left you there smashed into a thousand fragments, alone.

16

She was not to wait for him in the usual place, Luis had written on the little sheet torn from his notebook, she had read the message with a tight knot in the pit of her stomach, fighting back the tears, standing in the attic she has already collected her things, has taken a last look at the picture over the bed and started towards the stairs, towards the outside once again, leaving, but lingering on the staircase, stroking the chipped paint on the bannister, she goes slowly down, his words running through her head, 'don't worry, take care of yourself, please, we'll meet again,' but she does not believe it, completely alone, her eyes full of tears gaze through the window at the red flower pots in the courtyard, at the geraniums in the pots and beyond them at the end of the cloudy afternoon while she repeats 'these few lines to say a hasty goodbye' which he wrote rapidly with the blue biro, his writing almost illegible, the dots of the i's over the wrong letters, the words almost coming off the page, biting his lower lip and staring at her as she stares back at him from the head of the bed, 'we'll meet again', she reaches the landing on the first floor and stops in agitation as if she had run hundreds of miles up endless flights of stairs, pauses for a moment and sets off again for the street. She burned the message and did not take her eyes off the flickering tongues until the last letter blackened and turned to ash, 'we both know', she reached the door, took her coat off the hook, walked out, headed for the corner, turned in the direction of the avenue and disappeared into the crowd.

17

He had always dreamed of an island, of going to live on an island for ever. He wanted to walk along an endless beach of white sand with the pure blue sky reaching his heart, his skin tanned, his hair bleached, the sky cloudless, the palm trees near enough to touch, the sweet-tasting breeze, he had always dreamed of it. In front of him there opened up a stretch of stones, scrub and cactus, a deep ravine where the sun beat down implacably and where no rain fell for seven months on end; besides, it was summer and even the lizards were hiding behind the rocks. Beyond, the plateau stretched away into the west, to the interior, rising up towards the glaciers. The air was motionless; the only faint sounds were the old sandstone rocks crumbling into a fine, dead dust and the buzzing of flies around the carcass of a goat. The two men sought the scanty shade of an overhang of rock and sat down heavily, shaking the dust off their trousers and wiping the sweat for the thousandth time from their faces.

An island, then, he thought, a blue wave breaking on the sand, the gentle breeze rippling the water, the smell of brine mingling with the sweet perfume of tropical fruits. But above all the vast ocean, that huge patch of colour modulating from green to violet, to blue, white, yellow, the sea which insinuates itself into memory. He took a drink from the canteen and lit an old, badly rolled cigarette with hard paper and shreds of tobacco mixed with the hairs off a corn cob, breathed in the thick smoke and blew it out in rings which vanished into the midday heat. They had done a week's forced march and two days earlier they had left the dense jungle and entered the dry plain where the road to the high mountains and the route to the passes on the border began. They had lost their way and now they were steering with an old compass which misled them and sent them several degrees away from the true north they were searching for; when the night was clear and they were not overcome by sleep among the rocks and stunted bushes, they steered by the stars. Their feet were blistered and their shoulders lacerated by the continuous chafing of the straps of their rucksacks, the rifles beat against their backs and the butts dug into their ribs and the uneven ground forced them to climb, to scramble like goats up incredible cliffs with the sun drilling their heads and the heat climbing with them, overtaking them and lying in wait up above with a thick dusty blast which swept around the summits of the small peaks. From far off they could see an endless grey geography, an immense grey rock furrowed by thin trickles of water which disappeared into the small desert which looked like a saffron mosaic at the foot of the great mountain range. And there they were, two dwarfish shadows moving across the crags, always to the north, wandering, always towards the island which El Alto imagines with a gesture, a motion which memory brings back to him in the crown of a palm tree lashed by a tight rain and a raging, thundering sea in the midst of this silence, of this sun, of this torrential calm which feeds the vultures, the lonely raptors of the sierra.

Montero had built a rudimentary trap with which he hoped to snare a rabbit or a lizard, maybe a wild partridge or a vizcacha. It was getting dark and the sky was turning red behind the last mountains, the fire reflected in the desolate peaks. It began to get cool; a light breeze, which was already blowing up into a cold wind and would later rise to a freezing gale which made them close their eyes and hide their hands in the pockets of their green jackets. The fire was slowly heating a blackened saucepan where the soup was thickening into a sort of yellowish puree, which they nevertheless gulped down, with precise movements, chewing everything right down to the last scrap left on their tin plates. An enormous rabbit had destroyed the trap, eaten the bait and hopped away among the scrub and Montero swore that it had been laughing. Hence the old, thick soup, and the few dry crusts that they had managed to collect days before in a wretched shack at the foot of the sierra; sitting shivering in the threadbare blanket, he returned to the island, disembarked in the little bay, lay down to sleep on the sand and dozed off in the inhospitable creek, his bones aching, the unceasing wind, his body slumped against a few stones which provided a precarious shelter, dreaming of the sailing boat rocking like a feather on the water, near the white sand, a few yards from a man resting under a great green palm, with a heavy army coat and a rifle leaning on the trunk of a tree.

18

At this time of day the countryside is asleep, sound asleep beneath the hazy sunlight on the metal roofs and on the broad pastureland. A cow chews the cud while a little bird pecks the bugs off its back; a hoopoe flies over its nest hidden somewhere among the alfalfas and lands far away to throw the enemy off the scent – the hunter, the egg collector, the afternoon poacher who cannot sleep the siesta and strolls out into the yard while Javier and Carlos go round the dairies with their grandfather, climbs up to the windmill to throw stones at the pigs and ducks and to stare out towards the road which leads to the village. Suddenly he sees her, a blue dot moving along between the high paradise trees beside the road, the short, sleeveless dress, and the sun reflected in the white hair ribbon, in the plaits, in the tiny figure of Teresa who stops, takes off a sandal, shakes it until the stone falls out and walks on while he starts to climb down from the mill, jumps to the ground and says he saw nothing. Montero has prepared some watery coffee with the last few beans, ground with the butt of a rifle against a stone, which warms the stomach for the next stage of the march, a last glance backward and you run out on to the road, open the gate and race alongside the fence frightening the ovenbirds and the hamsters, up to Teresa who has stopped by the lake and is watching a little frog jumping, the slow circles in the water, the stillness of the high reeds which creak as the two men jump across to the other bank and march on with their eyes fixed on the high mountains to the north, ten or twelve yards apart according to the strategy learned over long years of struggle, of interminable battles at every point on the map, two men who tread on the same stones and respond to the same alarms, who walk in step and breathe the same air and are like two children on a lonely road near a country town, in the afternoon with the frogs sleeping on the eye of the water and the windmills motionless, the sails motionless, the pigs wallowing in the mud and the house silent beneath the January sun.

19

The man went into the bathroom, left the door half open and ran an appraising eye over the plethora of bottles and jars on the little shelf under the great oval mirror, took off his slippers and underpants, put his gold watch down on a blue handtowel, turned on the hot water tap and then the cold, tested the temperature with his hand as it gushed out of the shower, glanced in the mirror at the reflection of a middle-aged man, slightly greying, with a large paunch and wide hips, hairless, bandy legs, surveyed a naked man and stepped under the jet of water, rubbing his body vigorously with a sponge and humming the first bars of a crude tango. He picked up the little nail brush and scrubbed the damp skin of his fingers, then soaped his head until there was a thick foam, a cascade of liquid talcum powder over his broad shoulders, over the mat of hair on his chest, washed his armpits and blew his powerful red nose furrowed with little blue veins that looked like threads of ink, turned off the taps, grabbed a yellow towel, wrapped himself in the thick material and stepped out into the middle of the bathroom, wreathed in steam, a scent of pine soap in every droplet quivering on the white tiles, he dried himself conscientiously, flexed his muscles a few times, ran his hand through his tousled hair, opened the door wide, watched the steam drift out and dried the mirror with a cotton glove. He put on a pair of pale blue pants, dusted his little fat feet with a deodorant talcum powder, sprayed his armpits with a fine mist of lavender scented anti-perspirant, combed his hair with the thick part of the comb, gazed once more at the image of the familiar face in the mirror, walked out of the bathroom to the bedroom and dressed slowly, making each gesture a perfectly executed manoeuvre, a model of geometry and beauty, put on his impeccably polished shoes and said to himself, well, off to work, the night is young and you've got a difficult job, the kind you like. A long hard job in cold rooms with dim lights, flaking walls, the reek of urine and vomit, in cellars where the sounds of life in the streets were barely audible, familiar sounds of a car horn, the shouts of a news vendor or a sudden squeal of brakes and a yell of anger.

The enormous building seemed bigger in the darkness, the powerful searchlights swept the streets with blinding white light, the loneliness of a sleeping suburb at three in the morning. The high towers rose up to a starry sky; a few windows were still fainly lit by desk lamps or blue fluorescent strips and the whole structure looked like a strange insect getting ready to devour the shadows. He greeted the man on guard at the huge iron and glass door, took the lift and pressed the button for the sub-basement, lit a cigarette and loosened the knot of his tie. A long corridor led him through a series of identical doors, symmetrically closed behind their patina of dark brown varnish; he opened the last but one and before closing it made out the naked outline of a body lying on a bedstead, the arms and legs spreadeagled, the face covered with a blindfold. 'Evening, how's it going tonight,' he greeted them as he took off his jacket and left it folded neatly over the back of a chair. He walked up to the naked man who was about twenty-five, slim, his body bent with the cold and the position he was in and damp from sweat and the water that the electric train had carried again and again over every inch of his brutalized skin; he stared at the hands pressed against the sides of the body. 'You'll talk, they all talk sooner or later,' he told him, 'I can wait all night, all week, all your life.'

20

He collected the crumbs that were left on the table, arranged them in a little circle and placed a lentil which had fallen from the plate in the centre, leaned back in his chair and looked at it. In the kitchen she had plunged a glass into the soapy water in the sink and was washing it with a crumpled, tattered cloth, standing by the window that gave on to the garden, she looked like a teenager concentrating on a vital task, a teenager worn out by dreams that never came true and others that she would never even dream now, by brilliant projects that became dimmed year by year leaving her with a sad expression, a melancholy answer to the gaze of the man in the dining-room. 'I'm going out for a walk,' he said, 'I may stop by at the bar for a chat or a game of billiards.' He put on his check cap, his old leather jacket, felt the first gust of wind as he opened the door. Outside, the landscape was flattened by the frost; snow had covered the road and he could see a few tracks leading to the river, the tracks of wild dogs scavenging for carrion and of little animals fleeing from the dogs. He crossed the road and walked along the tiny path of sunlight that seemed to peter out at the end of the lane, quickened his step and went along Martin Garcia towards the park, dodged a bicycle that almost ran him down and entered the solitude of the empty benches and dry fountains, chose the usual spot and sat down on the freezing concrete surface, looked up and saw the great storm clouds forming on the high peaks, huge black stains on a sky empty of birds; he walked on in silence. Montero had stayed in the hut where they had arrived with the first shadows of evening and now he was repairing the transmitter, trying again and again to send words across the miles so that other words would come back to the abandoned shack in the middle of the winter mountains. He stopped by a tree bowed down under the weight of the snow and listened to the distant sound, a dog barking or a shout echoing off the high walls of the mountains, he hoped. The spout of the little fountain was broken and a careless sparrow had built its nest within reach of a child or an idiot, the twigs were interwoven with bits of cotton, paper and an incongruous thread of red wool. There were two eggs and he was surprised that the female was not there; the cold will kill them in the shell, he thought. He waited a moment to check where the sound was coming from, cocked his ears in the direction of the hut and heard only silence among the trees, the wind whistling, almost down on the ground, nothing else, but he did not move. The storm clouds were coming up now like smoke from the stack of a gigantic railway engine; they were clustering right over his head and blotting out the tiny eye of the sun, it's going to snow, he said to himself, and the eggs will crack open as if they were made of saliva, I'd beter take them home and put them in with the canary and see what happens. He stood up, made a small hollow in his scarf and placed them carefully in their new blue and green tartan womb, left the park and set off back to the house. Montero looked at him questioningly. 'All quiet on the front,' said El Alto, 'I thought I heard something but I think it was the wind or the glaciers breaking up in the distance, how's the transmitter?' He put the rifle down by the little wood stove that by some miracle was still working and helped himself to a mug of cocoa, sat down by the window and lit a cigarette. After a while he dozed off with the cigarette still alight in his fingers. The cold was more intense and snow was starting to fall slowly. He opened the door, put the scarf down on the kitchen table, took off his coat and took the two eggs out of their warm shelter. He brought over the cage with the canaries, hollowed out a rudimentary nest of wool and twine and placed it in a corner of the cage. The canaries glanced at it and carried on eating lettuce. 'They'll never hatch,' she said, 'the female's old and the male will peck them to pieces any minute, he's a mean old devil.'

21

Numb, he opened his eyes and calculated the distance from the narrow camp bed to the shadows by the door, his glance brushing the pale surface of the damp walls. How long had he been there, a day, two days, a week, years, what did it matter. A permanent fog blurred his notion of time, played tricks on him as he scuttled round the peeling walls, crushed him between the uneven bricks and the huge wet stains of urine and misery. He was no longer hungry and had eaten nothing since then, since they threw him in here, unconscious and alone while the pigs stayed outside swilling gin and guffawing, their shirts unbuttoned and their bodies poised to begin again on the ancient ceremony of pain. He crossed his bare arms over his chest, sore from blows and burns, and managed to create a little warmth. A trail of dry blood led to his navel, marking the route followed by the torture, a narrow path haunted by childish terrors of waking unprotected in the middle of the night, crows flapping around a staggering figure who refuses to fall, the appalling loneliness of being naked and tied to the cold springs of the bed, in the burning presence of an insatiable carnivorous buzzing. He drew up his legs and returned to the initial foetal position, the omnipotent nirvana of six months old, suckling at the luxury of his mother's breast, sipping from that spring which now seemed as far off as the cracked ceiling where the spiders and cockroaches lived, as far off as the memory of a summer in Santa Clara, his bare feet among the rocks lapped by a violet sea, the warm sun of early March, the little village sleeping in the symmetrical routine of its salty days, its old wood eaten away by saltpetre and rain. He touched his ribs gently and discovered an inflamed area, a great circular bruise over his heart, a stabbing pain whenever he pressed the blackish skin, maimed by a burning cigarette and dead ash. He stretched slowly, heard his joints creak, felt as if his body no longer existed below the knees, that it was just an extension of the shadow in the enclosed night of the cell. He imagined his legs but he could not see them; he did not dare to touch them but he knew he had drawn them up before, or had it been a reflex action that brought no result, just a long caravan of unladen camels in the immensity of a desert four yards square; he stretched out a hand and touched a foot, then the other, they were still there, he said to himself, deformed by a couple of fractured toes, but they were still there and if they are there the road is there as well, the chance to go beyond this nightmare, the horizon outside the bars, the house in the distant suburb, the café, the men in the billiard hall, and Marta will be there with the food ready and the table laid with the red and white check table cloth, the children's laughter, the winter evening outside the windows, the rain, this tear.

22

In July the sierra begins to freeze, the wind runs wild among the peaks and the animals take shelter in their lairs, the birds migrate in great flocks in search of the warmth of the north, the rain thickens and turns into heavy snow, white clods that fall open on the brown earth or hang from the branches of the petrified trees. The low shrubs are crushed under the white blanket; the fragile stems of the reeds rise above the snow like the masts of a foundered ship, motionless lookouts on an immense sailing boat aground in the silent, frozen storm. There appears to be one single cloud smothering the sky from the last ravine to the first step of the hostile mountains; grey and high, the cloud stays through the whole winter discharging its load of ice, its atrociously cold air, its eyeless gales against the defenceless slopes of the range. Everything stands still in this tormented landscape; no sound of the great birds among the stony peaks, no trace or sign on the narrow paths drowned in snow or on the fallen trunks. Only the wind plays music in the passes and on the plateaux, sole master of the stones, it races hemmed in by the towering walls of ice and carries away the thin column of smoke spat out from the chimney of the hut. An old wooden structure leaning or fainting against a rocky overhang that threatens to collapse on top of the snow-lashed roof. The black chimney looks like a crow perched on the precarious planks, its wings folded around the smoke that rises from its ashy feathers. Inside, the heat is barely enough to dry out the damp in the air, the smoke blown back in by the stubborn wind mingling with the sweet smell of mule flesh floating in the greenish broth, the hard potatoes not yet ready to break out of the skins, and the aromatic herbs that El Alto carried in his rucksack and which now form a dark layer on the surface of the stew. On the improvised table there are two dented tin plates and two opaque metal mugs, a long, hard old loaf, a few walnuts rescued from the snow, a desolate banquet for two men trapped in the harsh mountain winter.

23

An immense silence hung over the morning. The house could barely be seen among the trees; the air was suffocating and the sky almost white above the slow flight of a few birds. The windows were shut and two cars were hidden in a narrow lane covered with dry yellow leaves, the engines still warm, the windows wound down, a man dozing at the wheel of one of them, a fly buzzing around his thick breath. Inside the house, a few pieces of furniture failed to fill the yawning space enclosed by walls whose paper was peeling off with the passage of time, an irregularly shaped room with three doors leading to three other rooms; a glass partition around the ancient paraffin stove; a tiny fourth door leading to the cellar where people were shut up in little wooden compartments like animals kidnapped from the light outside, which burnt the countryside and dried up the water in the ditches. Their faces were covered by blindfolds which pressed on their eyes and left barely enough space for them to breathe the damp breath of the others, to eat their way slowly through the thick slop that they were given once a day; they were beaten as they ate, their bare feet broken, but they made no sound, no complaint, in the desperate knowledge that this meal might be their last and if it was not there was another day and they had to eat, to devour it all in order to imagine that day had come with the slowly growing heat in the permanent darkness of the cellar. He did not know how many of them there were, he had heard two of them speak and supposed that there was a third on his left, a stifled groan that reached his ears from some twilight zone and nothing more. There could be seven or ten or a thousand, but the silence was far more numerous. He remembered the journey from the prison, his hands cuffed behind his back, his back on the hard surface of the boot of a car, the uneven road, the call of a peewit, the unmistakable sound of a windmill swallowing the wind, the smell of freshly cut alfalfa in the gringos' field, the yellow butterflies which would die in the radiator of grandpa Salerno's old Ford T, Teresa's yellow skirt at mass on Sunday. Then they took him out and two of them carried him inside a house, rolled him down a long flight of stairs, shut him in a sort of wooden box and left him there, boiled alive, wounded, parched and alone in the middle of the night behind the blindfold. Then he saw her, her hair freshly combed, in white shoes, she walked into the church looking at the floor and clutching a little spray of jasmine which he had cut in the priest's garden, crouching between the rose bushes and the honeysuckle, his heart pounding like a galloping horse's, terrified by the nearness of the graveyard and the dark shadows of the paradise trees. 'They're for you,' he had said to her, 'I want you to take them to church tomorrow and put them for the Virgin, ask her for rain, grandpa's desperate for rain, he says the sun is going to kill all the plants, all the animals, that the river's going to dry up and so are the wells, ask the Virgin and don't say anything to Luis and Carlos, I don't believe in those things, ask her for grandpa.' And when she came out of the church without the spray you knew that was it and it did not matter whether it rained or not, she had done it for grandpa and you ran off through the charred cornfields churning up the earth with the straps of your frayed sandals. And the next day the rain came, poured down on the countryside and drowned the cocks on the weather-vanes, flooded the low fields of the big farm, swelled the narrow stream into a torrential river that even threatened some distant houses. The rain came in a cloudburst, a gigantic eruption of noise into the flat quiet of that summer morning and he heard it, at first it was like a tap dripping in the sink, then like a muffled murmur passing through the leaves and moving the earth like a tongue. Then he was sure, it was bucketing down and the water began to filter through the porous walls of the cellar, drop by drop onto his bare shoulder, running down him like a slow tide, soaking the cornfields, leaving the road to the farm like soup.

24

She thought of Javier and condensed her thought into a single image that went beyond his delicate, angular face, his broad shoulders, his long, slightly bandy legs. She thought of his open smile and the wind that ruffled his hair and filled it with sand in the high dunes that ran along the beach forming a yellow barrier crowned with dry bushes in the suffocating summer heat. They had put up the tent near the cliff and next to a natural well that gave them cold clear water, the two of them alone on their honeymoon down south on the endless coast where they walked to the crab pools and lay down on the rocks worn away by the sun and the storms.

She tried to settle in the narrow space left by the other bodies dozing beside her, stretched her arms and felt the lacerating pain of the handcuffs on her slim wrists, turned her legs towards the wall and breathed slowly out towards the darkness and the silence, towards the oppressive shadow swaddling the pile of bodies, wounded, soaked in sweat under the implacable sun that lifted little blue clouds off the surface of the sea, veiling the noonday light and dispatching the crabs to their afternoon slumbers. She fixed her eyes on the distant window and counted the seconds, then the minutes, closed her eyes and leaned her head on the cold tiles of the wall. A cool draught slipped round her neck and momentarily relieved the pain in her shoulders, the skin reddened by the sun and the iodine, merciless in January, 'You'll be scorched if you don't put your shirt on,' Javier had told her but she felt good like that, naked in the warm breeze that was like an immense caress which lulled her to sleep between the murmur of the surf and the mewing of the gulls and she awoke violently as the thumbs squeezed her nipples and the blows were distributed scientifically around her body, the hand that almost tore her hair out and lifted her in a single spasm of pain and dropped her heavily like a mirror smashed into a thousand pieces, the electric snake dancing madly between her legs and feinting a penetration that was never consummated, but which left its marks on her sex, her anus, and then crawled up to her mouth to bite her palate, bury her teeth in her brain, dry up her saliva, drag the screams from her soul and plunge her into a bottomless abyss where other birds were eating up her eyes and her tongue.

She woke up with a dry mouth and an urgent need to plunge into the water to calm the flame that was burning up her body like a napalm hand; she ran down to the waves and dived quickly in with a splash that took her down towards the smooth pebbles on the seabed. Seen from the beach her head was a golden stain moving away parallel to the reef with a short, dry stroke and a strong, even kick, hardly an occasional break in the line of the horizon. She stopped, panting for breath, her cheeks slightly flushed, looked towards the beach and saw Javier's blue trunks standing out against the almost white yellow of the sand, the high walls of the dunes and the narrow road to the village, and started back. She came out of the water with a wonderful feeling that flooded every corner of her pink skin, ran to the rocks and flopped down on the canvas, lifted her head and looked again at the little window that halted the air between the bars and filtered it drop by drop turning the atmosphere into a thick steam that fell on them all like a shadow, dripping through even onto the flagstones and settling in a stinking pool that was slowly asphyxiating them. 'Javier,' she said, 'come on, you'll be fried alive if you keep sleeping in this sun, Javier,' she shouted, 'where are you, for God's sake, I need you.'

25

The wind raced on through the narrow alleys of the sierra, whipping up a murderous icy dust which it hurled against the stones, whistled through the slender trunks which still resisted the terrible frost that gnawed away at their roots, stopping suddenly when another wind met it head on among the dead ravines and forced it back, choked by its own breath, its own frost. Perhaps it was the same wind that blew around the low peaks and then retreated like an invisible animal to spring out again, to make another attempt to flee along the deserted slopes, the stunted white crags, interminably.

El Alto had gulped down the thick black broth, the spoon had touched the rusty bottom of his mug to scrape up the last warm crumb of bread and the last pieces of the old vizcacha, had licked out the last bittersweet drop as the wind raged by the hut, threatening to sweep it away along with the four rotten planks that barely held up the roof. Montero was poking the fire in the grate, pushing the burning logs so that the smoke tried to escape through the chimney only to be blown back down into the room to the accompaniment of coughing and cursing from Montero, who refused to be beaten. 'You look like a smoked Buddha,' El Alto told him, 'sitting there like a statue, leave it, it makes no difference, it's too fucking cold to warm the place up with a bit of green wood.' 'I know what I'm doing,' answered Montero, 'wait and see, we'll have a nice little fire here in a minute.' At that very moment, Javier heard the door open and the clatter of footsteps coming down the stairs, felt arms lifting him roughly off the floor, pushing him so that he tripped, forcing him to stumble upstairs. They were taking him out of the cellar and he felt a stab of heat and points of light through the blindfold. He was back in the boot of the car, the terror was beginning again, the same bumping against the hard, dusty floor, perhaps the same streets and suddenly a different smell, sharp and salty, a smell that he associated with another landscape and with an immense blue colour. 'The sea, could it be, this is the smell of the sea,' he thought.

Now it was another place, his hand touched a polished, symmetrical surface, a hard wooden floor that was moving, rocking gently. At first he thought he was dizzy, he had not eaten a crumb for several days and the walls of his stomach were as close together as the walls of this strange prison cell that was swinging like a pendulum. 'I'm in a boat, they've put me in a boat,' he muttered, talking to himself, unable to understand what he was doing in a boat like this, beaten, weak, his eyes covered by a blindfold that made him lose all notion of everything. 'But I'm in a boat, I'm sure, that's a siren and I can hear the engine of a tug chugging or perhaps it's a little fishing boat sailing home.' Then he realized that he had another chance, they had not killed him yet. It was just another place to keep on waiting, only a thin wooden bulkhead between him and the seagulls and certainly a porthole up above him. They watched it pass by from the beach. 'It's a frigate,' said Marta, shading her eyes with her hand, 'or Captain Flint's galleon,' you answered. When it had dwindled to a dot on the horizon they had gone back to the tent to drink maté. Evening lingered among the dunes and a strange silence hung over the crab pools, 'Let me make the maté, yours comes out weaker every day,' you had told her. And now you imagined that you were there, in that same dead frigate, anchored in some tropical bay with a cargo of dubloons and fine silk destined for the cellar of a one-eyed man with a wooden leg. You smiled at the cruelty of the imagination, leaned against the edge of the bunk and stared into the distance, to where the blindfold stopped you like a precipice, you saw her barefoot on the sand, her hand over her face to keep the sun out of her eyes, her body firm and tanned, her fair hair bleached, farther and farther off, everything.

26

That evening, that evening in high summer, they had stopped on the bank of a sparkling river that meandered among the stones and he had watched the plants raising their heads above the surface as if watching the passing clouds, the birds flying by, the goats trooping slowly past as they cropped the grass in the deep ravine. A plume of yellow flowers crowned a thick brownish stalk which seemed to float suspended above the brown bed of the stream. Further off they could see blue and white patches stretching out like hands trying to touch the bank. The bustling peace of the mountain streams recalled his father's words, the little dams in the sierra, his memory filled with images of watercress and huge iguanas sleeping on the stones; he remembered his father peeling a branch with a penknife and the gentle buzz of bees around the honeycomb, a whole world contained in the memory of a siesta while two brothers waded up the stream searching for minnows to catch in a broken jar. That was how it had been, crystallized in the perfect shape of a petal lapped by the water, sitting on the damp grass with the merciless sun beating down in the summer air. He jumped up and realized that a strange silence had invaded the street, he went over to the door and turned the handle, barely had time to see them smashing the glass and bursting into the corridor firing their weapons and barking orders that ricocheted off the ceiling like the bullets. He jumped out of the window and ran to the staircase that led to the terrace, climbed up, stumbled, fell on to the warm flagstones and saw the bullet shatter the cage where the canaries were just a heap of crumpled feathers. He sprang over the Funes' wall and tore on down the long passage praying that they were not waiting for him in Santacruz Street, practically vomiting the lunchtime pizza, opening the screen door and out into the garden. In the garden he picked up the fishing rod and the jar of worms, fetched Javier and they set off for the brook; it was drizzling and a thin veil of mist covered the high mountains fading them into an illusory distance which he covered at full tilt and reached the passage. The blue snout of a lorry poked around the corner and then a thin black barrel, questing and spitting bullets which almost hit him as he dashed across the street in an attempt to reach the waste ground, 'If I make it to the trees, they'll never catch me,' he thought.

A flower that he had never seen before floated by downstream, he stretched out a hand to save it from the water and saw the slow dance of the minnows swimming around the bottom of the broken jar, heard his brother saying that he was going to scare them and turned his head expecting a bullet to blow it apart at any moment. But he did not see anyone, he was in the mountain, safe among the hot stones where the iguanas slept their slow siesta like dwarf dinosaurs, between the scent of peppermint and the buzzing of the bees, safe with his brother walking back from the stream with a pile of minnows for dinner, safe now in another bitter winter evening in the hut lost in the middle of nowhere, the snow up to the windows and the warm smoke leaking out of the blackened stove, the withered, faded flower which he still kept in the pocket of his tattered jacket, a water flower that had died long ago like his father, like the distant landscape and the drizzle, in the same way.

27

He was not going to tell them anything, nothing at all, how could he tell them where or when, he was already played out and his skin was worth less than one of the flies crawling over the leftover food, far less than the match that was burning slowly down under his fingernail, far less than the agony of burned flesh or the sickening stench of scorched blood. He would not talk, not now, not ever, the rules of the game had been laid down centuries ago, there is always someone who beats and someone who is beaten, helpless, tied to the wooden chair, blinded by light and impotence, disarmed, alone, abandoned, a piece of shit. But he would not talk, he would not say a single word to this bastard who reminded him oddly of a schoolmate years ago in his home town. The same ruddy face, the same fair hair and dead blue eyes, the same expression like an animal startled by the hunt, a peace-loving father, affectionate husband who goes to mass on Sundays and confesses his sins with the same regularity as he goes to the lavatory and drops his appalling load of corpses. But it is not him, it is a machine programmed to organize a gradual journey towards the last frontier of pain, a journey with no arrival, you are never allowed to arrive, never, programmed without pity, with the strange perfection of a gearbox moved by its own paleolithic instinct. 'Spit it out, come on, spit it out once and for all, I want to know where they are, I want to know if Salerno's in town and you're going to tell me if I have to burn you up to the elbows, or would you rather have a little game of roulette, hey Cardozo, pass me the 45, the gentleman wants a bit of fun.' Then he takes the magazine and loads it back into the butt, aims right between the eyes and pulls the trigger, gently, the fly tries to free itself from the sticky trap and leaves one of its legs glued to the quince jam. There is a metallic noise, dull, empty, and a guffaw from the blond, his teeth uneven and decayed, his breath steaming hot against your face when he tells you that you've been saved for the moment but he knows other tricks, an inexhaustible repertoire of inducements that will turn you into a scream, a single scream that will be lost in the dark passages, in the crumbling catacombs that have held you since that July morning, since that rainy morning when a car tore you off the pavement and four arms dragged you down into this other world that people do not know about, which they prefer not to know about as long as life goes on as usual a few feet above on the same pavements where people run for buses to arrive at work on time, punch the clock and start up the routine of surviving this chaos, this progressive destruction of everything. A few feet above, separating this hell from the immaculate offices where fates are decided, the fate of this gesture of closing your eyes, gritting your teeth, not screaming, not speaking, even though it's the last thing you do in the few minutes you still have left.

28

The light was barely visible against the thick curtain of water, sketching the damp landscape of the morning, the blurred profile of another day between ghostly trees and spongy ground. He walked, almost groping his way, to the outline of the bush and stopped, breathing in the strange odour of the soaking leaves, the laboured perspiration of the roots struggling for life in the mud. He unzipped his fly, held his warm wrinkled sex in his left hand and urinated on to the water, water on water, yellow on the dark brown of the bark. The rain would keep on falling and the days would become an endless succession of flashes of lightning against a grey sky. The hut no longer offered them protection from this infinite storm that seemed to grow inside the walls, chastising them occasionally with sudden gusts of wind that shook the stones and brought the cold in fierce, ravening flocks. He looked into the distance where an unceasing thunder reminded him of the presence of the stream which by now would be a raging torrent sweeping the last traces of the sierra away with it, a violent caress that drinks the rotten roots of the trees and the trailing nests of the great birds that seem to have flown away for ever. He felt the dampness of the air around his sex which rested on his left thigh and he also felt the hand sliding upwards from the knee, gently grazing the hairs on his leg, the nails leaving an open path for the lips and the saliva moistening his testicles, climbing on towards the hard tip trembling uncontrollably like a lookout perched precariously on the deck of a ship whipped by a hot wind and a tongue that starts to draw it into the darkness of the mouth. He sat up on the sheets and stroked the head that rose and fell, clamped to his flesh like a shipwrecked sailor, pressed it to his belly when the spasm opened the way from abyss to summit, breaking between his teeth like a wave on the stones of the beach. He stayed still for a moment and started back to the hut, lay down on the pillow, saw the thin plume of smoke rising from the chimney, lit a cigarette and asked her if she wanted to smoke, tore off a wild onion and put it in his mouth, she blew smoke rings, felt herself falling asleep and lay down with her back to him. He opened the door and saw Montero trying to fan some life into the fire, heard her ask him if he was asleep, 'The stream's swelling too much,' he said, he heard the bath tap, 'I don't like it,' he added. He closed his eyes, the noise of the cistern blended with another roar, 'We'll have to get ready to move on,' said Montero.

29

To ask *him* about Salerno, to try to force that name from *his* lips with a street, a house, a dark room and a camp bed. To try to make *him* sketch the scene where someone might be resting or keeping watch through the window on the silent night beyond the street corner and the dim lamplight. To talk about Luis to these butchers playing cheat in the next room and discussing their adventures in detail, their bestialities on waste grounds and embankments by the river, beside the black cotton-trees of the massacre. The wire around the corpse's neck, the heavy stone that will carry it to the muddy river bed for the catfish and the crabs, the anonymous body that will never appear in the newspapers and the tears of the people who will never give up searching for him or her in the interminable corridors, at the heavy desks where the papers pile up with false data and fictitious events, in the great theatre of offices full of lies and pious smiles. Where are you, dear Luis, has your adventure among the frozen slopes of the north come to an end, are you sitting under an old tree resting your long legs in the shelter of the stones of the mountain. You will remember as I do all the distance that separates us from Colonia Requena, the fields crowned with corn, your grandfather's stories. Teresa and Javier, the long siestas hunting for lizards, to the distant call of the hoopoes and the slow creaking of the windmill. How can I talk about you to those men banging on the table with the king of spades in their fists and shouting 'I want four, fuck it', before they go back to their job at the slaughterhouse, how can I confuse the toad Derby's with your name inside these filthy walls that echo the screams of a thousand throats that have faded into silence and the destiny of an unknown grave.

How can I exchange my pain for Teresa's eyes which were always on you while we suffered from the certainty that we had not been chosen for her affection and her golden plaits, let them go fuck themselves, my dear friend, my comrade, let them go rot in hell because they could never understand that pact made by three friends at the bus stop opposite Don Simon's shop one dusty January afternoon with the sun searing the roofs and the sadness of a goodbye that we had never dreamed of. You at the window and Javier and I waving our hands and fighting back the tears, trying not to speak your name now that the beating has started again, trying to imagine that the fight goes on, that you are there sitting in the shelter of the rocks with the same sad look dwindling into the distance down the road that separated us for ever. How can I shatter the memory with your name, how can I?

30

If only I had a point of reference, just one, a sound, the song of a bird or the noise of a car, anything. The place seemed like a safe, hermetically sealed by a little door which she had been forced to crawl through, banging her head on the upper frame, in darkness behind the blindfold which they had taken off later and she saw that she was not alone, that there were ten or fifteen women sharing a sort of mezzanine with her, a low roof and several tiny windows like ventilators and a long row of fluorescent lights that were permanently switched on. The light eventually became a new torture, a systematic white dagger stabbing into the brain and eating up sleep, memories, the memory where Javier, Luisito and Ana lived, the only place where she could still take refuge with a certain lucidity, the only geography she could still recognize as belonging to her, which they had not succeeded in wrenching from her in spite of the conscious disintegration that they had prepared for her little country of far-off affection and tenderness, for her tiny world that now seemed like a broken toy abandoned to the mercy of the scavengers. The little door opened twice a day and a uniformed guard brought them a ration of food which some gobbled down and others barely touched with their broken lips, which she ate slowly with her mind fixed on the obstinate notion of survival, to keep on with the laborious task of examining her hands, her legs, her body, pausing at the wounds that were beginning to heal, at the birthmarks on her shoulders that she caressed vigorously to confirm the image that she had of herself and that she had to preserve even at the risk of her movements being discovered from the spyhole in the door and punishment allotted in form of deprivation of food or an express prohibition that the prisoner, 'that fucking bitch', the phrase that she had heard ad nauseam, was not to go out to do her business in the stinking hole at the end of the corridor. That is not the worst, she thought, the worst is the uncertainty, the impossibility of resignation because one can see no destiny, no minute beyond the one going by now like a lizard crossing the flagstones of a courtyard. The worst is not knowing whether I shall be here tomorrow under this light, with these looks that pass from face to face seeking an answer to the question that no one has formulated but everyone has guessed, the worst is knowing that the door has opened and they have taken away number nine and she still has not come back and perhaps she never will, definitely she never will and her place will be taken by another with the same look, the same question, the same certainty of not knowing anything, the same recollections hidden in the memory like a safe conduct to a future just the size of a square with two children chasing the pigeons.

31

He woke early. The light was beginning to filter through the window and the first sounds were rising from the street to the room in the guest house, a twelve by twelve space in which the bed occupied the whole wall with the window and the ancient wardrobe with its three compartments completed the sordid, depressing furnishings. He stayed a long while in bed, lit a cigarette, then another, tried to draw the stains on the wall in his mind, the strange faces that stared at him from the flaking ceiling, the silent provinces that he could make out on one side of his shoes, between the crumpled, discoloured socks. He followed the course of a thin trail of dust up to the skirting board and let his gaze wander back to the frayed edges of the bedspread that had barely protected him from the intense cold during the night. He put out the cigarette in a glass that still contained a drop of gin, sat on the edge of the bed, yawned twice, ran his hand over the stubble on his face and started to put his trousers on. Once he was dressed he went out into the corridor and walked to the bathroom, switched on the light, looked at himself in the mirror, turned on the tap and let the brown water run until a light yellowish colour convinced him that it was no use waiting any longer. He washed his face, his ears, his neck, damped his hair, dried himself with a handkerchief and then urinated in the basin because the lavatory was not working and the smell at that time of the morning turned his stomach. He went back to the room, picked up his jacket, put on a scarf, went over to the window and stared for a few moments at the grey roofs outside. A woman was hanging out her washing on a balcony and the cold had turned her hands blue. He left the room, locked the door, went downstairs and was greeted by a blast of cold air in the street. He huddled inside the precarious protection of his jacket, pulled his scarf up around his ears and headed for the corner where the misted windows of a bar invited the passers-by to warm his innards with a large coffee and a couple of croissants fresh from the bakery. Coffee with four sugars, he told the waiter, lit the third cigarette of the morning and started to drink the black liquid which gradually spread its warmth through his body, buttered a croissant and bolted it down, waited a few moments and polished off the second with the last mouthful of coffee. He ordered a gin, made himself comfortable and eyed a blonde who was reading a book at the counter. He paid, stood up, passed by her and said, 'Beauty does not grow old,' the girl looked at him in amazement and he walked on out again into the cold of the morning and headed for the bus stop. He strode over a couple of puddles and had reached the pavement on the other side of the road when the car started to come round the corner and a few shops were pulling up the metal blinds and preparing to begin on the daily round. He thrust his hands into his pockets and lengthened his stride, the car was approaching the kerb and a group of boys went by kicking a tin can and hitting each other with their satchels, leaving the first marks on their spotless overalls. He looked up and saw a car braking beside him, the back door opened and two men with dark glasses seized him by the arms, hit him on the head with the butt of a gun, pulled him into the car which skidded off and he fell into a bottomless limbo.

32

When the man reached the river the beach was almost deserted. It was a brilliant morning and the heat was beginning to press on his neck and his armpits, the sweat flowed like another river and dampened his crotch, sticking the material of his trousers to his thighs and buttocks, wetting his feet inside his sandals. He sat down on the sand, took off his shirt and trousers, left his sandals in the shade of a post and walked down to the water, waded in up to his waist and felt the muddy bed between his toes. He ducked under quickly, felt a cool tingling behind his ears, came to the surface and began to swim slowly towards the middle of the current, avoiding the giant lily pads that were floating downstream. He swam on and turned on to his back, his face to the sky as the sun went about its task of melting down the air. He closed his eyes and enjoyed the noonday moment, the warm water holding him up like an enormous hand, the light breeze making ripples beside his legs. he thought about the dawn of that same day, in the dark house on the outskirts of town, the silence among the walls and the washing lines, the car crawling along like a giant nocturnal insect, the kick at the door, the astonished face of Galindez, the black, 'We've come for you, you lousy nigger,' the scream of the wife and the punch from Carreño that sent her sprawling against the kitchen table, the expression on the black's face as he whipped him with the pistol, the light that came on for a fraction of a second in the house across the street and went off again instantly plunging the scene into blackness, black like Galindez who they dragged to the car, his blood leaving a secret trail among the worn paving stones. He thought of all that as the sun climbed over the island, in his mind he heard the shot in the railway siding, Galindez like a drunken puppet falling beside a rusty locomotive and the dawn breaking over the roofs of the abandoned wagons. He opened his eyes, looked at the dark fringe of the beach and started back, cutting through the water.

Now the sand had taken on the shape of multicoloured figures which appeared to be sleeping, young reptiles sunning themselves on the remains of prehistoric reptiles which had become millions of yellow grains, an infinite number of microscopic stones lapped by the water and carried through the world with neither order nor purpose, a great transparent shell, another desert beside a tear. He ran over the scorching surface and reached the whiplash of shade where he had left his things, picked up the towel and dried his hands and face, lit a cigarette and sat looking at the island blurred by the tenuous haze forming over the water. He inhaled deeply and blew out the smoke in a great cloud that would soon turn to rain and join the heavy storm clouds that were looming up in the east. 'East wind brings the rain,' he thought. He turned round and saw them. They were coming down the steps on the bank, fanned out, four men and a woman, the light bouncing off the metal of the machine guns in a thousand sparkling shards that vanished among the boats near the shore, the pistols trailing from their hands like motionless dwarves awaiting the caress on the trigger, the signal to become erect in the damp hand pressing them against the leg, the imminent shot.

He stood up and backed away towards the water, tripped over a tin can and nearly fell on top of a girl who was bronzing her beautiful chocolate coloured body, reached the edge of the water and dived for the useless shelter of an abandoned boat, the absurd shelter of a few rotten planks half submerged in the remains of petrol and yellowish oil. He tried to clamber up on deck in order to jump across to the next boat, which looked safer, ridiculously safe with its worm-eaten gangplank. He stood up on one leg and felt a lacerating pinch which scorched his shoulder, breaking the bone and throwing him back into the stagnant, dirty, final water. He turned his head and knew that it would soon be night, the sky was growing dark above the tree tops and a dry, devastating rattle lifted him on to the deck, pierced by a thousand pieces of lead he fell against the edge of the gangplank, slid back towards the water and disappeared in a bubble, as round as the cloud floating overhead, releasing the fine rain, a summer storm in a small country town beside the river.

33

The little path was petering out, disappearing among the stones and the weeds that hemmed it in relentlessly until it was no more than a trace, scarcely a hairline blending into the barren, monotonous plain. The whole landscape was the same, a symmetrical confusion of colours and slopes, of clustered crags crowned by motionless clouds, of old birds of prey with hard beaks and razor sharp claws wheeling in slow circles. Here was the deep ravine, the narrow gorge where winter was beginning its slow departure from the frozen ground. A pale sun shone intermittently on the slopes and the moist trunks of the small trees, the thaw could be heard in the distant rumblings like drumbeats, the shy spring unfolding the first leaves, the first signs of green on the branches, the air still cold on the face.

The journey was beginning again.

Montero was walking in front and his bent back was the only point of reference to follow, the other movement among the silence and solitude of the mountains, the heavy breathing transformed into a rhythm of perfect harmony, ever northwards towards the border, towards the infinite line separating this sky from that other country, El Alto thought, to start again, to continue the tireless struggle, totally involved in a history which is scarcely theirs, inextricably caught in a beautiful dream handed down from the naked Indian and the Conquistador pinned to a tree by a lance, devoured by ants in a remote country, in a fantastic geography that would kill him time and again although the defeat was there like an atrocious, unequal destiny, like a naked Indian, massacred and forgotten among thousands of corpses, beside the same streams that they were skirting now, tired and dirty, driving themselves on to the last step, the next exit, the next entry, again.

They took a rest under a jagged overhang and lit the fire, dropped their rucksacks and ate in silence, drank from the dented canteens and slept in the shelter of the great stones. They woke to the sound of cavalry, the monotonous clang of armour, the approach of danger. They glanced at each other for a fraction of a second and took up their positions with their ears pressed to the ground; motionless and alert they let them reach the little clearing that opened below, drew their bows and waited. A group of four iron men appeared around the little hill, tall and monstrous under their grey breastplates, the morning light glancing off the steel of their swords and twinkling like a thousand eyes on their silver helmets.

'We will kill them again and they will come back out of nowhere, riding their horses and hurling themselves into combat with their crosses and their banners. They will burn down the villages again, carry away the great sun from the temples, rape our wives and murder our children, day after day.'

Bow, arrow and hand were still in an exact, precise, final drawing. Then the drawing sprang to life and the invader fell pierced by a dart in the neck, in the leg, in the eye, while the fourth horseman fled, crouching over the saddle and ducking the low branches. They beat them to death with clubs; furious, they annihilated them with arms and memories. It was all over, the silence slightly disturbed by the hiss of the arrows and the quickly stifled cries of the dying, no more.

They put out the fire, picked up their rucksacks and marched on. The sun was already warming the afternoon and the clouds had disappeared from the incredibly blue sky which they would soon leave behind.

34

From a distance the landscape looked like a flat painting against the even grey of the sky, like a crowd standing on the horizon behind the fences, the same green summer surface, the country. The dirt roads fading into the hazy air under a glaring sun, a tractor ploughing the furrows from memory and the skeletons of the windmills watching over the water by the rusty tanks, the bleached corn, the cool, quiet barns, the sacks of grain piled up against the bricks where spiders and bats lived. In those days he thought that the world ended in the town, on Saturday evenings when the old lorry went round spraying the streets near the square and splashed mud on the women's spotless dresses and the men's freshly polished shoes. What more could there be than the matinees at the Rex cinema where Luisita Escudero swooned in the arms of Raul Marconi while the orchestra attacked the final bars of the waltz of the moment? What could an ungainly adolescent imagine sitting in the second row with his eyes glued to the celluloid city that rose menacingly with its high buildings and ceaseless movement? How could he get inside the skin of those people strolling along indifferently while the camera moved slowly away and the sweet vendors appeared and the footlights went up? And when everyone had gone, he stayed there alone, mesmerised, with an empty packet of chocolate peanuts, knowing that until next Saturday the week was taken up with boring maths lessons and milk deliveries to the neighbouring farms, a furtive cigarette on a deserted road, the chance of seeing Teresa on the way to town in her father's pony trap. Javier and Carlos would be waiting for him near the bowling club and they would go to hunt vizcachas together, smoking them out of their holes and trying to shoot them with their grandfather's 22 rifle so that their mother could pickle them. Everything waas exactly the same every day and the cinema was like a mysterious window from which you could see the far side of the moon.

'I don't understand why you want to go away, all your family are here, you've always lived in this town, your brother is going to be very lonely,' Teresa had said. 'Besides, you and Carlos and him have always been together, almost since the first day, and I'm going to miss you a lot,' she had added. 'I'll write to you, don't worry, and to them, Teresa, but I have to find out what else there is beyond all this. I feel as if I'm suffocating, I need to go away,' you had told her with a hard expression on your face to hide all the sadness you felt. 'I'll write to you every week, I promise,' you lied.

The handkerchief fluttered in the window of the bus like a crazy bird and the town was left behind, sunk in the deep calm of the siesta and they disintegrated into the dust like clay figures. Teresa had not gone to see him off because it was better that way, 'I don't want to start crying like an idiot with Javier and Carlos there, write soon, please.' He folded the handkerchief, squeezed it in his hand for a moment, put it in the back pocket of his trousers and followed the trail that Montero was hacking out with blows of his machete.

35

The black earth gave off a sweet smell of first buds, of embryonic roots. Sketches for trees and plants began to emerge from the silent hearts of seeds and laborious worms, the whole coast was a landscape being reborn. The river came languidly, came dark and silent to mingle with the deep salt of the ocean, reenacting a monotonous ceremony of infinite embraces and couplings. Through the wooden bulkhead he pictured it as a slow horizontal rain that would never stop, a melody exhausted in a single note, the only company apart from his memory. He had managed to get used to the ceaseless motion of the walls, the vomiting was less frequent and his head was beginning to clear away the slender spider's web of the first day's sailing on the spot. His eyes had adjusted to the sticky darkness as if they were two bats sleeping on either side of his nose, the tenuous drop of light that managed to penetrate the inside of the prison allowed him to survey the body stretched out below his gaze over and over again. It was like looking at oneself with a dwarf lantern, like exploring a cavern by the glow of a match. His hand wrote a name in the void, drew the face of a name on the damp wall, his fingers spelt out Marta on the edge of his lips but did not manage to name the children, he refused to bring them into the heart of the nightmare, they were just a memory frozen at a precise moment of any given day and fixed to the wall with invisible drawing pins, like a photograph. The two of them in a park or in the country, happy and beautiful, just that, another memory could break him in two like a splinter.

Last night the screams had begun again. At first they came as if transmitted by distant voices, then it was a continuous wail that was only extinguished at dawn. 'They must have killed him,' he had thought, interrupting a winter afternoon next to a sparrow's nest in a desolate suburban square. 'You bastards, you're going to kill us all in this bloody mousetrap,' he had almost shouted as he walked home with two eggs inside his scarf. 'Any minute now they'll be coming back for me,' he had bitten back the words so as not to break the oppressive silence that followed the horror of the screams. He went on with the repeated task of recreating Luis' story, how he had constructed the new nest with kite string, he confused himself with Luis and saw the canaries eating their ration of lettuce, looked at her looking at him and saying that the canary was going to peck them to pieces, that the male was a mean bird and he knew that Marta would never have said that, that the pigeons would have hatched out in the warmth of an oven smelling of detergent and grown before the astonished eyes of two children who are now looking at him from a deserted beach in an invisible photograph.

36

A face stood out in the fog, the image of loneliness, a sort of escape from the light, a figure of desolation. He tried desperately to find an answer to this obsessive vision, tried to discover if it was really him walking away, stooping slightly, his legs bent as if his body was about to collapse. Only the night had the texture of a legitimate memory. For a moment he thought he was dead, that the last blow had sent him across the last threshhold, tht he had entered the void. An infinite calm caressed his bones and peace settled on his skin like a stork on a church tower. But it was not true, he was painfully alive, terrifyingly here. The world still counted him among its insects and his body recalled another night, the repeated questions, the old familiar faces behind the blows and the burns, in the hollow sound of the triggers being pulled, the empty chamber aimed at his tormented head, at a man walking on down the street skipping over the puddles between the uneven paving stones.

The same Carlos Lafuente, the same twenty-nine years, and yet everything was different, he understood that he was on the point of attaining his objective, a couple of yards separated him from a hole in the ground, an infinite fall into the depths with the fish. This time there was no escape, he had not fallen into the Carranza's tank, Don Cosme would not be coming to pull him out, half drowned and covered in slime. Teresa would not be standing there in the middle of the courtyard covering her face with her hands, there would be no sun and no scent of alfalfa, just a black burst of gunfire cutting off his breath and the letter he had never written would never arrive, 'Dear Teresa, I'm well, I've found work in an office and I'm studying at night. Life isn't as difficult as I'd expected, I haven't seen Luis yet, tell Javier that as soon as I do I'll tell him to write. I won't tell him anything about us, I'd rather things go on as they are. I love you and miss you.' He had never had the courage to send it and she was still the most beautiful memory of his life, the last stage of a memory that was associated with a round yellow moon over a sleeping countryside, a flight of ducks migrating south. This time it's finished, he thought, 'I love you and miss you,' the man said smiling, stooping even lower beneath the drizzle.

37

She walked like a drunk; her legs moved unbelievably slowly as if they were moving on their own, detached from the rest of her body. She dragged her feet and tried to avoid the pitfalls that she discovered in her path; she leapt time and again over towering walls and fell back on the same spot. She thought she would never manage to leave this flagstone and move on to the text, finally managing to advance the miraculous inch that would get her out of the trap. It was like trying to stand upright on two rubber stilts that doubled up with every step, threatening to dash her on the floor thousands of feet below.

She passed by her companion and back again; the chain went taut and lacerated her ankle and she started back, an infinite distance that was a yard long and was the only distance that was her own, the only reference in a space that belonged to her only tenuously and over which she moved like a pendulum counting the minutes and the seconds with her mangled fingers, the hours and the days with the dry blood covering her wounds, the symmetrical absence of nails. She took off her rough hemp sandals and let her feet rest slowly on the cold surface; swollen and deformed, they only became aware of the sensation of nakedness after what seemed an interminable time. Then she put her rough sandals on again so that the guard would not find out, so as not to add another punishment to the carnage, so that she could continue to circle around the girl huddled in her corner, hiding inside herself and whimpering like a wild animal. She had talked; they had beaten her and she had not opened her mouth, they raped her systematically and she did not utter a word, the electricity had brutalized her naked body, had broken her inside and out and she stayed dumb. They had staged a mock firing squad and her face remained impassive beneath the tears and the terror, they told her that her husband was dead, that they had made mincemeat of him over days and nights of appalling sessions of torture. 'Bastards,' she had managed to say before they raped her again, 'We've got your daughter,' they told her and she did not believe them, 'She's four, she's called Susana and she's blonde like you,' she had heard the harsh voice of the cruellest one say, 'You wouldn't like anything to happen to her, would you?' he had added with a guffaw.

Then she had talked.

She knew that they had beaten children in front of their parents, that they had tortured the mother and father in front of children who hardly knew how to talk. She knew the names of some children who had disappeared forever, they had killed the parents and then sent the children to other countries and sold them, or they had murdered them somewhere or other, banishing them from life with a single gesture, like swatting a fly.

Then she had talked.

Now she did not move from her corner and whimpered, whimpered, wept and whimpered; wept again and said 'Susana, Susana, my little girl, darling,' and started to weep again.

She sat down, put on her sandals, lay back against the wall and said Luisito, said Ana, said I know I'll never see them again. But she could not cry.

38

Falling sheer from the highest peak of the promontory the gully looked like a deep gash between the harsh slopes, a blemish on the profile of the sierra. The plain had come to an abrupt end in a compact chain of dark steps in the ground dotted with extinct volcanoes, ancient mouths that had sculpted the strange shapes of the stones. They were there now, 'Here we are and the journey goes on,' El Alto thought. He had almost forgotten the physiognomy of the cities, the monotonous murmur of the streets, the particular smell of certain places, the dirtiness of the air above the clustered buildings, the figure of a woman in an anonymous window. His life now was the path, the narrow goat track and the unending search for the elusive horizon. His life stretched from a suburban house to the next ascent along the knife edges of the abyss. He left behind the data of an urban biography confused with the aliases that concealed his clandestinity and his habits, his ways of life in a geography that disguised him in guest houses and impersonal rooms, his gradual detachment from the things that until then had made up his life. Then he began to classify his memories as if they were an indispensable collection of data, butterflies still fluttering in his mind. He carried with him a sleeping town and the countryside which began at the doors of the houses, the rusty signpost that said 'Colonia Requena 2 miles' at the side of a minor road, Teresa's astonished face which had followed him ever since that dusty afternoon, although she had not gone to see him off, Javier and Carlos' frayed sandals flying after a ball on the club ground, his grandfather sitting in the cool shade of the paradise trees, sipping a maté and scaring the flies away with his cane.

All this lived in his memory in an uninterrupted sequence of the past.

At times he was back on some corner in the City, sweat trickling down his back and the weight of the pistol making a bulge in his thick coat, the leaden sky and the fine drizzle blurring the skeletons of the trees and the figure of his comrade on the opposite pavement, soaking the car parked a few yards away with the engine running. At times he saw the man coming out of the doorway, pulling up his lapels and walking quickly across the street towards the avenue until a crossfire hurled him on to the wet pavement and the car disappeared into the safe delta of narrow streets and wide avenues. He could almost see the windscreen spotted with the huge drops of a sudden torrential rain and hear the distant wail of the sirens.

Here we are, he repeated, leaning on a great grey stone sculpted by the wind and the fire at the centre of the earth. There they were, fanned out, walking slowly down the steps to the river bank while the body that lay smoking a cigarette on the sand turned its head and suddenly understood that this was the end.

39

He imagined things, places, shapes that he had never seen and faces that he had never known. He imagined long corridors that would finally lead him to the light, the open air, the magnificent panorama of a sky that would enfold the whole planet. He had chosen to enter fully into the continent of the imagination, to pad out his recollections with the invention of a new memory that would carefully select new data, other seasons teeming with newly born creatures, on a journey strewn with the hope and despair of another stage, however short. He had the enormous advantage of a boat to travel across warm oceans to remote isles and coral fringed coasts. His cramped cubby hole resisted the onslaughts of violent tempests and protected him from the mindless sun of the tropics. The salt and iodine helped to staunch his wounds and he journeyed on steadily, peacefully, slipping through the waves like a dolphin separated from its brothers and suddenly falling into bottomless abysses with his body broken and his life hanging from a scream which was lost among the lily pads on the bank. When he steadied his course the questions and the blows began to drill into his brain again, his teeth loosened under the pressure of his jaws and the electricity burrowed fiercely into his testicles that were like two cracked, wrinkled raisins swollen to the size of two tangerines. Names, places, even a detailed confession with dates and clues that he did not even know about no longer mattered. It was merely a ceremony tediously prolonged under the cover of sultry nights filled with obscenities and preposterous stories of what they had done to Marta and the children, 'She's just shit, understand, a heap of shit in the arsehole of the world and you can say goodbye to the kiddies, get it into your head, they're orphans, and you don't exist either, you're a number, there's nothing left of you, if you talked it might be different, you've got nothing to gain, time's on our side and you know it. Your wife talked but there are still a few details that you can fill in, get it, you're a worm and we're going to keep beating the shit out of you till you tell us what we want to know, so talk.'

He crawled laboriously out of the faint and started to swim slowly along the reef towards the shore and fell exhausted on to the hard lice-ridden bed. If Marta had talked, what could she tell them, that Luis was her brother-in-law and that they had had no news of him for more than a year, that was all.

He tried desperately to keep imagining brilliantly coloured landscapes with palms and a warm breeze caressing the huge green leaves. He tried not to imagine Marta's body tied to a chair with her breasts mangled, her tremendous pain, in some part of the City, a broken flower beside a vase dead from thirst and darkness. Ana and Luisito were waiting for him by the abandoned boat, they had lit a little bonfire and were getting ready to cook the fish freshly caught from the sea, they looked like shipwrecked sailors, which is what they were, the only survivors of the shipwreck. Where are they, what has become of them, they're two children and they're alone, he started to swim strongly, kicking the hard bulkhead with his bare feet, striking out in the night like a blind man without his stick. I'll never get there, he thought, while they waved to him as they chased the seagulls along the sand.

40

The garden was not very large; it occupied the space in front of the house and was hidden from the street by a high privet hedge. A compact bed of geraniums occupied half of the adjacent wall and the rose bushes separated two paths bordered by poppies in bud and long stalks crowned by daisies of a surprisingly vivid orange. A few wild flowers clustered together beside the lawn as if for protection because they had sprouted from solitary seeds blown there by a caprice of the wind.

The man was sitting at an old iron table working skilfully at the transplantation of some dark bulbs from a small flower pot to a much larger one. His hands cleaned the slender filaments and sifted the dry earth which clung to the reddish sides of the two receptacles and a pair of enormous pruning shears rested beside a half drunk cup of coffee. The afternoon was hot and a storm was threatening.

A woman with dyed straw-blonde hair came out of the house and began to water the little shoots with a long, faded hose. 'Don't bother,' said the man, 'it's going to rain any minute and they'll have water to spare. Get me another coffee.' The woman turned off the tap, wiped her hands on her apron and went into the house; a rumble of thunder announced the arrival of the rain. A few minutes went by and the woman came out again with a pot of coffee and a clean cup. The man was finishing his task; he patted down the fresh soil and put down the pot beside an enormous shiny rubber plant, 'Get my bath ready,' he said, 'I'm going in at seven today.' 'Have you got a lot of work?' asked the woman. 'A bit to catch up on,' answered the man helping himself to two lumps of sugar.

He had a quick shower, dried himself on a yellow bath towel, flexed his muscles, put on a pair of light blue underpants, combed his hair with the thick part of the comb, walked out of the bathroom and into the bedroom, dressed meticulously, making each movement a perfect manoeuvre. His newly polished shoes were at the foot of the bed, he put them on, looked at himself in the wardrobe mirror and walked out of the room, kissed his wife softly on the cheek and opened the door to the garden. 'Try to get home early, the children are probably coming to lunch,' he heard his wife say as he plucked a dead petal off a rose and stepped into the street. When he arrived, it was almost seven and the rain had been falling on the city for a while, he showed his badge at the door of the building and walked yet again down the same corridors. He stopped at the same door, loosened his tie and went in. 'You here again,' he said, looking at a young woman lying naked on a bedstead with her hands tied and her legs open. He took off his jacket and went over to the woman. 'It's no good, kid,' he told her, 'we've pulverized your old man and we've got your daughter, that's right, she's four, she's called Susana and she's blonde, looks just like you.'

41

It made no sense but he remembered her with her hands smelling of garlic, a pungent aroma that seemed to come from her fingers and pervade the air like a little swarm of cloves chopped on the kitchen table. That's how it was, his memory of her was invariably associated with lunch and the hour before the siesta, the sudden silence of birds and machines, the hour for love, she used to say. When he wrote that note he knew that part of his life would always remain in the places where their little story had been written, the chronicle of a couple walking through a park kissing with their eyes open along the hidden paths leading to the fountain, just a few lines in tiny handwriting in the urban life story of two anonymous lovers, strangers in the same City. A minute later and it might have been catastrophe, terror suddenly present in the ordered geometry of her provincial habits. She had never known about the parallel life that he led in clandestine rendezvous, in sudden disappeareances which he explained away with journeys that he had never made. She believed him and he thought that he was not really lying to her, just drawing a thick smokescreen to cover any connection, any trail leading to her bright eyes, her name repeated over and over in the immeasurable loneliness of the mountains, that name that he sometimes confused with Teresa's because they had been the only women in his nomadic life, that name repeated in the midst of a silence that pierced the stones in the freezing nights of the sierra. 'Some day I shall have to go away, don't ask me why or when, you have to realize that I'm just a traveller, a bird of passage,' he had told her as they walked along the banks of the river. 'If the time comes, I shall write you a note, we shan't be able to say goodbye, you'll have to burn it when you've read it, it's very important for you to burn it.' Perhaps she had always known and her tacit acceptance was just a confirmation of the fleetingness, the repeated frustration of happiness and the beginning of pain. 'I only ask one thing, that you remember everything as I do,' and he agreed, he still remembered her with her hands smelling of garlic, her bright eyes fixed on some point on the island, the slow summer dusk in a gaze that went far beyond any words.

42

The sheets were hanging on the line, white, pure, spotless. Their grandfather told them that they had hung out to dry the ghosts that had wet themselves during the night because they had been playing with fire and they imagined a pile of ghosts sleeping and waiting for the iron to wake them up as it smoothed out their wrinkles and folded them at the corners, ready to be put away in grandmother's room. 'The next time you wet the bed, you'll have no pudding for a week,' their mother's voice feigned a severity denied by the calm expression on her pale face, by the sweetness of her look that embraced and protected them. It was the holidays and the days seemed as if they would never end, they stretched out over the fences and the gates, stopped to drink in the lakes and finally gave way to warm nights with a sky full of stars. The roads cracked in the sun and the soil was a thick blanket patterned with hoofprints and wheelmarks, and the hamsters scampered around by the ditches and hid whenever a tractor lumbered towards the Swiss cheese factory.

Their sweat still had not dried and a new blast of boiling air swept down on them, punishing them for venturing on to the arid plateau, the desolation reserved for lizards and scorpions and birds of prey with beaks of stone.

They wandered with their catapaults slung around their necks, their pockets full of little round pebbles and their eyes open for the peewits and finches flying low over the ground. Their sandals sank into the earth, sending up little puffs of dust, the wood pigeons lined up along the fences and flew away from the pitiless attack of the little savages. The stones bounced off the telegraph posts and the dull thuds echoed along the wires, reached the metal tip and spread all over his body biting the pores of his skin, digging into the marrow of his bones, filling his blood with monsters that savaged his brain from inside, driving the oven-birds from their round nests of dry mud.

Their strength was beginning to fail them and the road had disappeared beneath the gigantic slabs of limestone, the north was fading into the distant hills, their blistered feet were scorching inside the leather boots, the straps of their rucksacks dug into their shoulders and the sun crushed them with its weight until they were two drops of water about to evaporate.

They sat down under an enormous willow and cut the water melon that they had stolen from the gringo, bit into the red pulp, spat out the seeds and lit a cigarette that grandfather had left in his old grey overcoat. Evening lit up the horizon and the lorry passed slowly by in the direction of the town to water the streets around the square, 'Hello, Eustaquio,' they shouted to the driver, who waved back to them. Now it was dark and they were still five miles from the pin point on the map that indicated a pass over the massif, through his muscles that were tensed like springs 220 maddened volts broke his flesh without leaving a single wound, demolishing his kidneys.

They went back to the house leaving a heap of green rinds under the willow and a half-smoked, dried up cigarette hidden in a hole in the trunk, 'Luis, Javier,' they heard their mother calling, 'I've been calling you for an hour, come and wash your hands, dinner's ready.'

43

At least he knew something; it was Sunday.

The commentator's voice was describing 'the incredible atmosphere setting the scene for the eagerly awaited clash between these two old rivals', a sunny Sunday, the terraces packed with spectators and the flags waving behind the goals; 'Drink Monje, the vermouth for magic moments', the green pitch and the freshly drawn chalk lines, 'Ladies, don't wait till tomorrow to buy your fridge, look at the prices and go to Rocaferri Brothers today and choose the fridge that will last a lifetime', the tremendous roar that greets the local team as they run out on to the field 'with their famous red and white shirts, led by their captain, Mario Disanto, who's back today for the first time since his injury two months ago, looking as fit as ever', the hiss as the away team appear at the mouth of the tunnel 'led by veteran Carlos Miguel Clavero, the legendary centre forward who has taken this popular southern team to so many unforgettable victories', his hands are slightly less swollen and he can move his right leg, but he has a raging thirst, he has not had a drink for two days and his stomach feels like a burning coal; 'the players are lined up, everything's ready, there's the whistle and they've kicked off', the match had got all the pigs huddled round the radio, has transferred their violence from the broken bodies lying in their own filth to the obscenities hurled at the linesman or the blue and golds' defence, 'a brilliant move by the inside right, he crosses to the centre and Menendez misses an open goal, a sitting duck, the ball went miles over the top', at least they've taken off the blindfold, at least I can look at the wounds, see where I am, not that it's any use in here, in this ghastly half light, the damp walls and the dried blood, 'this game isn't coming alive, both teams are playing around in mid-field and then rushing away with the ball into the opposing half looking for an opening', somebody told me that the kid they brought in yesterday is dead, he was groaning all night and he's not moving now, he looks like a dog sleeping in the hallway, now he's free, you think, someone has finally managed to escape from this hell, you think, 'the home team are playing a bit better, but when the blue and gold forwards attack you can see the gaps in the back line, Romero just doesn't seem to be getting it together today', the commentator's voice comes clearly through the door, so do the pigs' remarks, the same voices that ask and insult and shout day after day and that have changed the script today and are yelling from a distance about the pathetic way their favourite team are playing, the same people who conscientiously break the defenceless bones of someone they have never seen before are getting excited today about ninety minutes of play, balls bouncing off the goalposts and unpenalized fouls, there's no solution to this madness, you think, what an appalling mess of shit these men must have inside their heads, you think, 'what a marvellous piece of play, he dribbled past three defenders, just the goalkeeper to beat and the shot just scraped the left post and went out', the shot had blasted his guts and he was exactly that, a dog sleeping in a hallway, motionless, he takes no notice of the flies and the unbearable stench that comes up from the covered grating, 'there's the whistle for half time, a match that quite honestly leaves a great deal to be desired, let's hope that the second half will give the thousands of fans who have flocked to the Carmelo Barrera stadium today their money's worth', just my luck, it had to be my turn on duty today, you hear one of the pigs complain, in a minute I'm going to go in there and make somebody suffer, you hear the voice go on, somebody is probably going to die to compensate for the frustrated football mania of a man who is sick in the head, maybe it will be me, maybe he's going to kick me to death just for being here, a Sunday afternoon, because it's Sunday, you know that and it's the only thing keeping you in touch with a reality that is falling apart, 'second half, Jesus Antequera has stayed in the dressing room and they've sent on Raul Carreño in his place, a junior with a bright future', let's hope they win the match, if they lose, these bastards will murder us one by one, the commentary comes through as a low muttering, they're going to murder us anyway, you hear someone answer, 'Torcali's coming forward, a deep pass to Ortega who runs into the area and falls, he was brought down just as he was going to shoot, it's a foul, an obvious foul, and the referee is pointing, there's no doubt, it's a penalty, but the rival supporters are leaving no doubt about what they think, either, they're throwing anything they can lay their hands on on to the pitch, one of the linesmen has just been hit by an orange', an orange, a beautiful golden orange rolling over the grass leaving a trail of sharp, cool delicious juice, you think, I'm dying of thirst and there are people throwing oranges around, 'fortunately it looks as if the linesman is okay and everything is ready for the penalty', if he scores, better for everybody, you hear the absurd comment from the shadows, better for who, you wonder, if we're all dead already, we're a pile of corpses just waiting to be thrown into the ditch, 'the referee is giving the final instructions to the goalkeeper and Cholo Martinez is placing the ball on the spot', life depends on a penalty, my God, I don't know whether to burst out laughing or crack my head against the wall till it splits open like a melon, 'he runs up, shoots and Albarracin stops it, a fantastic leap by the goalkeeper, springing like a panther and just reaching the ball, everybody ready to yell goal, but not this time', you hear the obscenities and the thumps on the table in the next room, 'twenty minutes left and the away team seem to be in charge of the match', twenty minutes separating life and death, this appalling agony of the final moment, today, Sunday, another of us is going to die, you think, a sunny Sunday with people strolling in the park and sunbathing on the beach, children flying kites against the blue sky, 'the home team have fallen back, they're playing for a draw, they're all over the place, a move on the right wing by Arriola who pumps a tremendous shot at the goal, Vazquez just manages to get a finger to it and pushes it away for a corner', in the next room the silence is absolute, you can imagine the pigs crossing their fingers and waiting for the dangerous corner shot, it's Sunday and people are going into the local cinema to see two films for the price of one in a cinema in town, old women are taking the air in the doorways of their houses and fanning themselves with magazines open at the horoscope page, you imagine, 'he centres the ball, the defenders jump but Oliva comes in like a tank from behind, a tremendous header that leaves Vazquez helpless, goal, goal, gooooooooal'.

44

She woke up, woke up again, tried to imagine that she was free between her eyelids and her pupils, in that minimal space, hardly big enough to contain a tear, she was free, she could stay like this, enclosed in this freedom until she could put the previous minute in order, the previous hour, the last week, the interminable month, the infinite months, the lifetime that had passed through her bones without Javier, without the children, since that night, since the first blows and the stupefying confirmation of a night-mare that grew before her eyes like an alien from another planet, before her eyes which had still not learned to enclose a second of freedom between the eyelids and the pupil. They would force her to open them, they would force her again, shaking her head as if she were a rag doll, they would tear out clumps of her hair like fragile stems, someone would rape her again, one more act within the immense tragedy that was being acted out in this other world, she would feel the brute's compulsive panting and the slobbering gasps of a cadaverous orgasm, she would hear the laughter of the others and the harsh insult of the frustrated rapist, 'sodding bitch, you can't even fuck,' and more laughter bouncing off the walls, and her eyes closed desperately to stop the tear from falling, her grief from overflowing, her disgust, her heart-rending loneliness through her eyelashes, towards the swollen cheeks, trickling down the misshapen, bloody lips, falling like a hunting trophy at the bastards' feet.

This time she would not open her eyes, she would bite her tongue to pieces before she opened them, they would put the electric filament in her anus but she would not open them, perhaps another brute would cover her with his sweat and his rage and his foul smelling sex, but she would keep a precise memory between the pupil and the eyelid, some memory that would unite the four of them in this wretched landscape. She could choose and nobody could prevent her, she could choose a beach or a wood, a rainy morning in the mountains or a sunny day by the crab pools. She could imagine Ana with her yellow sandals running around her grandmother's garden in Colonia Requena or Luisito hiding behind the armchair and playing at the invisible man, she could imagine Javier coming towards her on the other side of the road and waving to her. If she opened her eyes it would all disappear, they would be reduced to a fleeting vision which would become confused with the flaking walls and filthy doors. She would not open them and Luis would keep walking along some distant, hidden path, or along an anonymous street in an anonymous city. 'Luis Salerno, we want to know where he is, Luis Salerno,' the voice asks again and the blows start again, 'it's a matter of time, if you don't talk tonight, we can have another little chat tomorrow,' she would not open them, 'Your husband's already feeding the worms and the same thing will happen to you, but first we want to know where Salerno is,' she would not open them, 'you can start saying goodbye, the party's over, tomorrow is the last day, there's a lot of people queuing up for this bed,' she would not open them, 'you've got tonight to think it over and say goodbye to the other girls because you're already dead, you don't exist any longer, you're not even a number, you're nothing,' she would not open them and even less now as Javier opens the door and the invisible man jumps out from behind the chair and snatches the breakfast biscuits out of his hand.

45

Goodbye again, it was more a greeting than a goodbye, it was what he repeated every morning when he imagined that day had broken, when he suspected that somewhere the light was beginning to flood over places and landscapes, small rooms and immense prairies, a flagstone and the whole pampas, goodbye again now that a fleck of sunlight appears on the floor and I see it in my mind next to the door and it's coming in through a window the size of a fly, just enough space for the winter to come in and nothing else, goodbye again, night goes on inside the blindfold and my swollen eyes could not see a fleck of sunlight even if there was one, even if it smashed through the window pane like a stone, I'm almost blind and the only thing I can see is your body, the memory of your body like a bonfire in the middle of the desert, I say goodbye to you because I always say goodbye, because I don't know whether today will be the last day, I don't know whether today is tomorrow or if all this silence is hardly a second, the life of a butterfly, the beat of a hummingbird's wings on a flower, or a windy freezing year tht has stopped in some month or other never to move on again, that's why I say goodbye when I deduce that almost a day has gone by, because I don't know whether I'll be able to do it tomorrow and I don't want to leave, I wouldn't want to leave without greeting you from this appalling loneliness, from this platform hemmed in by damp walls with one foot on the step of a train that will never return, goodbye again, I don't know whether you're alive, I don't know if you've left, if they'll have let you walk out of this nightmare, if I'm talking to you at all really or to the memory of a skin that perhaps no longer exists, I know absolutely nothing, my brain is naked and my mind empty, only memory is left, the memory of you and one or two others, the children and my parents, Carlos and Luis and Teresa and a few more, it isn't much but it's enough to allow me to say goodbye, to wave the handkerchief in the distance, to say goodbye to you again now that it's day, now that it's night and the door is opening or I remember that the door is opening and I can see you far away with your bright eyes open, with your glance that passes me by but does not touch me.

46

They took their chains off and handcuffed them behind their backs, checked the blindfolds and yelled at them a couple of times before forcing them out into the narrow corridor which, he imagined, led to another exit, another cell, another appointment with the same performance of pain and extermination. He tried to count in his mind how many people were walking out of the hole with him and stopped at a figure that oscillated between seven and nine, plus one dead one who stayed spread out on the damp floor like a shadow dissolving slowly in its own putrefaction, like a dog asleep in a hallway. 'The kid's dead,' you hear the harsh voice of one of the brutes, 'one less,' you hear the reply, 'It's a good job we're leaving,' the conversation continues, 'This smell of shit is too much for anybody,' says the voice, 'A nice job for the gravediggers,' somebody laughs, 'or for the fish,' adds another. 'There's nothing like a bullet in the guts to sweeten the atmosphere,' now the guffaws fly up like startled crows. They force them to walk somewhere, hitting them with their pistol butts and kicking them up the arse as if they were cattle. The last journey of the last herd, that's it, you think, and this is the last stop. Now they are beating you on the back, 'Come on, fuck it, you mob of cunts, hurry up, we haven't got all day,' another blow.

It was a strange noise, the rasping sound of an engine in the distance and as they went forward it got colder, a draught of freezing air blew at them from somewhere and cut through them like a long dagger, body after body after body to the last skin in the line. And then the open air, the sun, the sudden brightness half guessed at behind the filthy rag, 'Up there is the sky, I'm treading on soft, wet earth, I can feel my lungs transparent, it must be a glorious day,' you think, 'it's a wonderful day,' you say in a low voice, 'and it's the last,' you add.

Now you know that the noise was the noise of a helicopter, that you're inside it, that it's climbing, that in a few minutes they are going to fling you through the door, throw you out head first into the void, straight down to the salt water that you can smell in the air, like a bird, wounded and suddenly and finally deserted by the secret of flight. He knew it would be his last journey and yet the morning seemed beautiful to him, it seemed beautiful to feel the air on his broken body, on his last sensation of being here, on this planet crushed by an ancient pain, by the same wound that they constantly reopened.

They must have taken off his handcuffs, they stand him up and he feels the wind whipping at his trousers. They have also taken off the blindfold and he can make out the blur of a blue space and a cloud of haze on the curve of the horizon. Yes, they have taken off the blindfold and let it fall at his feet as if it were his last gesture, this torn, dirty farewell falling to the floor like the body that falls stripped of all memory, covering in a few seconds a distance of years, a heap of bones against the metal sheet of the water.

He could not rid himself of a strange feeling or knowledge that he was being detained somewhere on some street, walking slowly towards a blind appointment which he knew absolutely nothing about, moving like a shadow through landscapes that changed abruptly from one street to the next. At times he thought there was too much light for a single sun in a sky that never grew dark, a transparent, empty sky that sometimes joined the earth in an illusory horizon, in a fine film of saliva where memory passed like a paper slipped under a door.

The only certainty was his solitude, his body leaning against the wall, sitting on the only chair in this half empty room, standing by the window which looked out on to the past, perhaps the other certainty. Only the past which arbitrarily linked the invisible thread of motionless fragments in a space which felt infinite and irrecoverable. His own name had blended into other names, confused in the spider's web of an indispensable anonymity, which he had thought indispensable then, and whose point of departure he was unable to define, the launching of a ship becalmed for centuries on an unknown, hostile coast. Since then a steep path had led him past crossroads which marked the exact place where all the creatures of his love rested, ceaseless ghosts that raked the earth, trying to call him, blurred faces that fell on him without compassion like birds fleeing from a fire.

Perhaps distance distorts history until it becomes an absurd and whimsical game where victory is hardly even a relative fact, a chance number on a board, where life and death become alternatives that have the same value as a dice spinning in the darkness, where that body, that voice and those eyes forever occupy a place banished from the world.

That was why he was alone, but he carried a multitude in his eyes when he looked inside himself and dropped off to sleep, clenching a hand that the air threatened to dissolve at any moment and turn to dust, snatching it away through the open window, scattering it among the shadows of the trees and leaving an absent shadow beside the bed. The strange music of the leaves was all the company he had, a subdued murmur that rose in pitch as it reached the upper branches and finally vanished at the top of a diapason of roots and bark, of thick sap through the wrinkled tree trunk of memory.

He went over to the window and looked towards the south, towards the night falling beyond the little garden. He stayed there for a long time, standing in a slow, leaden twilight and thought he saw, far off, two men running through the darkness, dodging fallen trees and low branches that almost whipped their faces.

I have to go back, he thought.